'Holiday romances seldom work out,' she murmured.

'That's what I've heard.'

'Keep reminding me that this is nothing more than a few weeks of fun, okay?'

Finn rubbed his jaw. He had to acknowledge that it would be easy to forget who they were and why they were here. They were on a fake honeymoon—emphasis on the *fake*—surrounded by romance and luxury, and they might easily get swept away and inadvertently slip on a pair of those rose-coloured glasses.

He—they—had to keep their eyes open, their heads in the game.

Callie turned her head and sent him a small, almost sad smile. 'We're on the same page?'

He rubbed his hand over his jaw before nodding briskly. 'Just to be clear—are you saying that you'll sleep with me?'

The tip of her tongue touched her top lip and he saw her skin flush with anticipated pleasure. Yeah, she would be his as much as he would be hers. Tonight.

Callie held his eyes as she sucked in her bottom lip. 'Well, sleeping isn't what we would be doing, exactly.'

Dear Reader

When I wrote THE LAST GUY SHE SHOULD CALL I got so many messages from readers asking for Callie's story. Something about the vivacious, independent, flirty character grabbed them, and—Callie being Callie—she hasn't stopped nagging me for her happily-ever-after since then!

When a condom falls from the pocket of a gorgeous blonde's jacket into his lap on a flight back from New York to Cape Town, travel writer Finn Banning knows that Callie Hollis is trouble with a capital T. She's bold and flirtatious, and somehow he finds himself in a discussion about his upcoming wedding and her feelings about love and marriage... She's cynical and sceptical and she doesn't buy into the concept of happy-ever-after. But Finn needs a wedding planner, and Callie gives him the name and number for her friend Rowan, who is doing just that.

Three months later the wedding is off and Finn finds himself all at sea. He's not particularly upset about losing his fiancée, but he is devastated at the loss of his dreams to have a family. He also has a huge problem in that he's been contracted to write a series of articles for an important publication on upmarket honeymoon destinations, to be researched while he's on his honeymoon, and he can't let them or the magazine down.

Nobody is more surprised than Callie when she finds herself agreeing to act as Finn's fake wife. But needs must: she needs to vacate Cape Town to avoid meeting up with her mother, who left her and her brother Seb when they were very young, so she jumps at the chance to spend three weeks with the über-delicious Finn Banning at various luxury honeymoon destinations in Southern Africa.

It's a perfect arrangement—she'll be his rebound girl and he'll be a fling, and in three weeks they'll wave each other goodbye. *Hmm...I don't think so!*

I hope you enjoy Callie's story as much as I loved writing it.

Happy reading!

Joss xxx

Come and say hi via Facebook: Joss Wood Author or Twitter: @josswoodbooks or visit www.josswoodbooks.com

THE HONEYMOON ARRANGEMENT

BY
JOSS WOOD

MILLS BOON

First published in Great Britain 2015
by Mills & Boon, an imprint of Harlequin (UK) Limited,
Eton House, 18-24 Paradise Road, Richmond, Surrey, TW9 1SR

ISBN: 978-0-263-25722-9

Joss Wood wrote her first book at the age of eight and has never really stopped. Her passion for putting letters on a blank screen is matched only by her love of books and travelling—especially to the wild places of Southern Africa—and possibly by her hatred of ironing and making school lunches.

Fuelled by coffee, when she's not writing or being a hands-on mum, Joss, with her background in business and marketing, works for a non-profit organisation to promote the local economic development and collective business interests of the area where she resides. Happily and chaotically surrounded by books, family and friends, she lives in Kwa-Zulu Natal, South Africa, with her husband, children and their many pets.

Other Modern Tempted™ titles by Joss Wood:

PROLOGUE

'MINIMALISM, MODERNISM OR IMPRESSIONISM?'

Finn Banning looked up from his seat in business class into the lovely face of a navy-eyed blonde with her hand resting on the seat in front of him. A ten-second scan told him that her body was long, lean and leggy, her waist tiny, her bright blonde hair falling way past her shoulders. Another five seconds of looking into those impish flirty eyes told him that she was Trouble. With a capital T. God, he hoped she wasn't sitting next to him on this long-haul flight back to Cape Town from JFK.

Over the past two months his life had been turned upside down and inside out and he didn't want to make small talk with a stranger—even if she was supermodel-gorgeous.

But he couldn't help the corners of his mouth kicking up in response to the mischief in those amazing eyes.

'Graffiti,' he replied when she cocked an arrogant sculpted eyebrow.

Her mouth twitched in what he suspected was a smile waiting to bloom.

'Whisky or bourbon?'

'Beer.'

She tipped her head and tapped her foot, encased in what looked to be, under the hem of dark jeans, low-heeled black boots. 'Rugby or cricket?'

He'd never played either as he'd spent every spare moment he had at the dojo. 'I was on the UCT crochet team.'

Her mouth twitched again with amusement as the other eyebrow lifted. 'You went to the University of Cape Town? Me too! What year? Degree?'

'Journalism. Is there a point to these questions?'

'Sure. I'm trying to decide whether you're worth flirting with or whether I should ignore you for the rest of the flight.'

She flashed him a megawatt smile that had his groin twitching and his heartbeat jumping. An elegant hand gestured to the empty seat next to him.

'My seat.'

'Ah...' he replied. Of course it was.

Finn watched as she tossed that bright head of relaxed curls and pushed some of them out of her eyes. Reaching for the strap over her shoulder, she dropped her leather rucksack to her feet and shrugged out of her thigh-length brown leather coat to reveal a taut, tight white T-shirt that covered small and perky breasts. *Nice.*

She folded the coat and stood on her toes to push it into the bin above their heads and that white T-shirt rode up to reveal a tanned, taut stomach and a beaded ring piercing the skin above her belly button. He watched, bemused, as she picked up the leather rucksack, pulled her tablet and earphones from the bag and tossed them on the seat. Holding her rucksack in her hand, she pulled a shawl from it, and as the bag tipped a thin, familiar silver foil packet fell out of a side pocket and landed on his thigh.

Finn picked up the condom and held it between his thumb and forefinger, waiting for her to look at him. When she did, instead of giving the blush he'd expected, she just flashed him another lightning bolt smile and nipped the condom out of his grip.

'Whoops! Maybe I should introduce myself before I throw prophylactics in your direction. I'm Callie Hollis.'

'Finn Banning.'

She wasn't shocked that he wasn't shocked, Finn thought as she tucked the condom into the back pocket of her jeans. Then again, after eight years as an investigative journalist before switching over to travel journalism nothing much shocked him any more. He'd seen the worst of what human beings could do to one another and, since it wasn't the first time he'd had a condom tossed in his lap by a beautiful woman, it didn't even make a blip on his radar.

Callie brushed past his knees and dropped into the seat next to him, wiggling her butt into the soft cushions and letting out a breathy sigh. She was all legs and arms and he would bet his last dollar that she hated economy class as much as he did—at six-two, for him it was like trying to sit in a sardine can—and that she figured the ridiculous price for a business class ticket was worth every cent.

Callie dropped her head back against the seat and then rolled it in his direction. 'So…married or single?'

'Why does it matter?' he asked.

Callie grinned. 'Well, I do this flight every month or so, and it's been a *looooong* time since I've had someone sitting next to me who I'd want to flirt with—normally my travelling companions are old, dull or ugly. And besides, when the guy is as hot as you flirting is fun—and I'm really good at it.'

He had no problem believing that and told her so. 'It must be because you're so shy and timid,' he added, his tone super-dry.

Callie laughed—a deep, belly laugh that made his stomach clench and his groin jump. 'That's what my best friend Rowan says all the time. Anyway, we were talking about flirting… If you're single you get the full treatment. If you're married I behave like a normal person.'

'I'm in between. I'm engaged.'

'Pooh.' Callie pouted. 'Well, your loss—because I flirt really, *really* well.'

He absolutely believed that.

Callie wiggled in her chair again, and tucked her legs up and under her. 'So when are you getting married?' she asked, and he could see that she'd dialled back the charm.

'In three or so months' time.'

She fiddled with the clasp of her seat belt and looked at him, puzzled. 'I don't get the whole marriage thing. What's your reason?'

Finn stared past the lovely face to the darkness beyond her window, frowning when a quick, instinctive answer didn't fall from his lips. Shouldn't that be a minimum requirement when he was contemplating spending the rest of his life with someone?

Her question raised all the issues that he'd been struggling with lately. Were he and Liz doing the right thing by getting married just because Liz was five or so weeks pregnant? It was the twenty-first century—they didn't need to get married to keep living together, to raise a child together. Were they complicating an already complicated situation? It wasn't as if their relationship had been fantastic lately, and he was mature enough to know that a baby was hard work and might put more strain on the frayed rope that was keeping them together.

On the other hand, being parents might bring them closer...

God—a baby. He was still taking it in. He wanted to be an integral part of his child's life and he was excited about becoming a dad. Maybe the birth of his own child would fill the hole that had appeared in his life when James died three months ago. A birth for a death, it seemed...*right*.

Fitting. Fated.

Finn rubbed his jaw. He was approaching his mid-thirties

and he wanted to be a brilliant father to someone. James had been one to his stepbrothers, to him. He wanted to create a family of his own—something he'd only truly experienced when he was fourteen and he and his mum had joined the Baker gang—a single dad and his three sons. He wanted to be part of something bigger than himself and he and Liz had been good together once. Maybe they could be again. Actually, they didn't have an option. They *had* to make it good again.

'So, why are you getting married?' Callie asked again.

He frowned at her, warning her off the subject. 'None of your business.'

Callie's low chuckle floated over him. Warning ignored, then.

'Of course it's not, but I'm always fascinated as to why someone would be interested in tying themselves down for ever and ever and ever...'

'Love?'

'*Pffft*. That's just an easy excuse—a myth perpetuated by movies and books.'

'You don't believe in love?' Finn asked, intrigued despite himself. Because, deep in his soul, he wasn't sure if he believed in the fairytale version either.

To him, love was taking responsibility, showing caring, companionship and loyalty, and he firmly believed in those. Besides, Liz hadn't got pregnant by herself, and if he was part of the problem then he would be part of the solution.

Right now it seemed that marriage *was* the solution.

He saw something that he thought was sadness flicker in Callie's eyes.

'I believe the only pure love people have is for their children, and some people don't even have that. No, love is a generic term we use to feel safe. Or comfortable? Possibly co-dependent?' Callie suggested, twisting in her seat as the aircraft started to move down the runway.

'Is that what you see love and marriage as? Co-dependency?' He couldn't believe that he was having a conversation about his upcoming marriage with an absolute stranger. Reticence was his usual style, along with reserve and caginess. He *asked* the questions, dammit, he didn't answer them.

Callie shrugged. 'I think that a lot of people use love and marriage as an escape from whatever is dragging them down. Just like some people escape to drugs in order to feel happy, others escape to love.'

Whoa. He was occasionally cynical about love and relationships, but she made him look like an amateur. He was cautious, thoughtful and rational about the concept. He took his time to become fully invested in a relationship and he never made quick or rash decisions. Which was probably why he was feeling so out of sorts about getting married—he hadn't had nearly enough time to think the whole situation through, to process the changes.

And he was still dealing with the death of the only father he'd ever known. Finn pushed his fingers to his right eye to stop the burning. Would he ever get shot of this ache in his heart?

Callie placed the tips of her fingers, the nails shiny and edged in white, on the bare skin of his forearm. 'Sorry— I'm being an absolute downer. I'm just naturally sceptical about love, marriage and relationships. It's a crap shoot and I'm not much of a gambler.' Callie bit her bottom lip. 'I admit that I'm a little too outspoken and opinionated—'

He couldn't help his sarcasm. 'A *little*?'

'Okay, a lot—but I do wish you happiness and success.' She tucked her foot up and under her backside again, and sighed theatrically. 'Both my brother and father—neither of whom I thought would *ever* get hitched—are getting married within the next couple of months, so I'm going to have to learn to keep my cynical mouth shut.'

Despite having only known her for twenty minutes, Finn knew that was impossible.

'Thank goodness that Rowan—my best friend, who is about to marry my brother—is an event planner and she's organising both their weddings. I just have to show up and look pretty.'

Pretty? She could don a black rubbish bag and still look stunning, Finn thought. Those eyes, those cheekbones, that pink tongue peeking out from between those plump lips... He wondered what she would taste like, how those breasts would fit into his hands, about the baby softness on the inside of those slim thighs...

Whoah!

What the hell...? Rein it in, bud, before you humiliate yourself. You're engaged, remember? An almost father, an about-to-be husband.

Knowing that she'd said something of importance that he hadn't picked up because in his head he'd been tasting her skin, he mentally rewound. 'Wait...you say your best friend is a wedding planner?'

'Mmm. Actually, she does all sorts of events, but she's great at weddings.'

'My partner—fiancée—is going nuts. Apparently there isn't a wedding planner in the city who'll take on organising a wedding at the last moment.'

'When are you getting married...tomorrow?'

'As I said, we'd like to get it done in three months or so.'

Liz wanted the wedding done and dusted before she started to show as she wasn't comfortable displaying her baby bump to her conservative relatives.

'And finding a wedding planner is something I have to do in the next couple of days.'

'Why isn't the bride-to-be looking?' Callie asked. 'Shouldn't that be her thing?'

'Liz is in Nigeria for the next six weeks, so finding a wedding planner has become my job.'

'What's she doing in Nigeria?'

God—more questions. He didn't think he'd met anyone more inquisitive and so unreservedly blatant about it. *So, Sherlock, why haven't you shut her down yet?*

'Liz is a consulting engineer working on an oil rig.' He saw her open her mouth and held up a hand to stop the next barrage of questions. 'This friend of yours...the wedding planner? Is she any good?'

Callie nodded. 'She really is. She started off by doing kids' birthday parties and then she did a Moroccan-themed wedding which was amazing. In eighteen months she's done more than a few weddings.'

'Can I get her number?'

'Sure.' Callie nodded. 'If you allow me one last word on marriage.'

'Can I stop you?' Finn raised a dark eyebrow. 'And just *one* word? How amazing.'

Callie ignored his quiet sarcasm. 'It's not from me but from Nietzsche...'

Good looks and good brains too? Callie was quite a deep little package.

'Nietzsche, huh? Do enlighten me.'

'He said something about love being many brief follies and that marriage puts an end to said follies with a single long stupidity.'

Huh. Some German philosophers and some navy-eyed blondes were far too smart for their own good.

'I need a drink.'

Callie grinned. 'People frequently say that when they're around me.'

Finn didn't find that hard to believe. *At all.*

CHAPTER ONE

Three months later...

CALLIE, ABOUT TO pull the door open to their favourite watering hole, the Laughing Queen, frowned as Rowan held the door closed and stopped her from walking inside.

'What?'

Rowan narrowed her eyes at her. 'Can you try and remember that this is a *business* meeting? That my client and his fiancée have called their wedding off two weeks before they were supposed to say I do. Do *not* flirt with him!'

Callie, purely to wind Rowan up, flashed her naughtiest smile. 'Why not? Maybe me flirting with him will cheer him up.'

'Don't you dare! I swear, Cal, just behave—okay?'

'I always behave!' Callie protested. Okay, that wasn't true, so she quickly crossed her fingers behind her back. For most of her adult life, whenever she'd found herself back in Cape Town, she had normally ended up in this bar, getting up to some mischief or other. Jim and Ali, the owners, loved her because she always got the party started and they ended up selling much more liquor than normal.

'Just no dancing on the bar or impromptu line-dancing, okay? Or, if you have to, pretend that you don't know me.'

'Hey! I'm not so bad!'

Rowan was thinking of Callie's early twenties self, or

maybe her mid-twenties self…maybe her six-months-ago self. The truth was that it had been a while since she'd caused havoc in a pub. Or anywhere else.

Normally, whenever she was feeling low or lonely, needing to feel outside of herself, she headed for the nearest bar or club. It wasn't about the alcohol—she'd launched many a party and walked out at dawn stone-cold sober—it was the people and the vibe she fed off…the attention.

So why, after a decade, was she now boycotting that scene? Had she totally lost every connection to the wild child she had been? That funny, crazy, gap-toothed seven-year-old who'd loved everyone and everything. That awesome girl she'd been before everything had changed and her world had fallen apart.

Sadness made her throat constrict. She rather liked the fact that at one point in her life she'd been totally without fear. That was how she usually felt in the middle of a party she'd created: strong, in control, fearless.

Maybe she should just start a party tonight to remind herself that she could still have fun.

When she repeated the thought to Rowan, her mouth pursed in horror.

'You are hell on wheels,' Rowan grumbled, letting go of the door handle and gesturing her inside.

'And *you* were a lot more fun before you got engaged to my brother,' Callie complained, stepping into the restaurant. She waved at Jim, who was standing behind the long bar at the back of the large harbour-facing restaurant. 'What happened to my wild, backpacking, crazy BFF?'

'I'm *working*.' Rowan said through gritted teeth. 'This is my *business*.'

Seeing that Rowan looked as if she was about to start foaming at the mouth, Callie slung an arm around her shoulder. 'Okay…chill. I'll behave.' She couldn't resist another dig. 'Or at the very least I'll try.'

'I was nuts to bring you along tonight,' Rowan complained, leading them to an empty table in the corner and yanking out a chair.

Callie took the seat opposite her and flipped her hair over her shoulder. Seeing Rowan's irritated face, she realised that she might have gone a little too far, so she placed her hand on hers and squeezed. When Rowan's eyes met hers Callie met her dark eyes straight on. 'Relax—I'll behave, Ro.'

Rowan scrunched her face up and when she opened her eyes again let out a long sigh. 'Sorry. It's just that I feel for this guy. I mean, can you imagine calling it quits so close to the wedding?' Rowan picked up a silver knife from the table and clutched it in her hand. 'What could have gone so badly wrong so late in the day?'

Callie heard the unspoken question at the end of Rowan's sentence. *And what if it happens to us?*

'Easy, Ro. Seb adores you and nothing like that is going to happen.'

'Bet Finn didn't think that either,' Rowan muttered.

Finn? Callie stared at her. Finn Banning? The guy on that flight back from JFK? The one she'd never quite managed to forget? The one she'd recommended Rowan to as his wedding planner? Black hair cut short to keep curls under control, utterly mesmerising grape-green eyes and that wide-shouldered, long-legged, slim-hipped body. The man who had starred in quite a few of her night time fantasies lately.

'Finn? You've got to be sh—' Callie caught her swearword just in time. With Rowan's help she was trying to clean up her potty mouth. And by 'Rowan's help' she meant that she had to pay Rowan ten bucks every time she swore. It was a very expensive exercise. 'You've got to be *kidding* me.'

Rowan placed their order for a bottle of white wine with

a waitress before answering her. 'Sadly not. Anyway, he's the strong, stoic, silent type—not the type of guy who you can commiserate with. So don't let on that you know.'

Of course she wouldn't. She was loud and frequently obnoxious, but she wasn't a complete moron.

She had a low-grade buzz in her womb at the thought of meeting Finn again—jilted or not. She still had a very clear picture of his super-fit body dressed in faded jeans, his muscles moving under a long-sleeved black T-shirt, sleeves pushed up to his elbows lounging in the seat next to her; his broad hand, veins raised, capable and strong, resting on his thigh. His quick smile, those wary, no-BS-tolerated eyes...

She had amused him, she remembered, and that was okay. He'd looked as if he needed to laugh more. And, more worryingly, those hours she'd spent with him were the last she'd spent in any concentrated, one-on-one time with a man.

Maybe she was losing her mojo.

'So, how long are you in the country for this time?'

Rowan changed the subject and Callie sighed with disappointment. She wanted to gossip a bit more about the luscious Finn.

As a fashion buyer for an upmarket chain of fashion stores Callie was rarely in the country, constantly ducking in and out of the fashion capitals of Europe and in New York and LA. Trips back home were rarely for more than a week or two—three if she was at the end of a three-month rotation. Wasn't she due for a three-week break soon? Hmm...she'd have to check.

'I'm flying out to Paris in a little while and will be away for a week.'

'Aren't you sick of it, Cal? The airports, the travelling, the craziness?' Rowan asked. 'I could never imagine going back to my old lifestyle, kicking it around the world.'

'But, honey, you stayed in grotty hostels and hotels. I travel the easy way—business class seats, expensive hotels, drivers, upmarket restaurants and clubs.'

Rowan had been a backpacker—a true traveller. Callie wasn't half as adventurous as her friend; unlike Rowan she'd never visited anywhere that wasn't strictly First World.

Upmarket First World. She was that type of girl.

Callie frowned. Rowan had a look in her eye that told her that she was about to say something she wouldn't like. She'd been on the receiving end of that dark-eyed look many times since her childhood and she leaned back in her chair, resigned. 'I know that look. What's wrong?'

Rowan pulled in a long breath. 'I don't know... I'm just concerned. Worried about you.'

Callie fought the urge to roll her eyes. 'Why?'

Rowan stared down at her hands. 'Because...um...'

'Jeez—just spit it out, Rowan,' Callie said, impatient.

Rowan's eyes flashed at her command. 'Well, okay, then. Seb and I are concerned because we think you might be becoming...what's the word?...brittle, maybe.'

What? 'Why?'

'You gobble up life, Cal, like nobody else. You love people and you talk to anyone. Within two seconds everyone adores you and wants to be your best friend. You are the only person I know who can walk into a party and within half an hour have everyone doing shots and then the conga. Men want you and girls want to *be* you.'

Well, that was an exaggeration—but it was nice that Rowan thought so. 'So where does the worry and the brittle part come into it?'

'Being bubbly and funny and outrageous has always been a part of you, but we sort of feel like you've been acting lately. It's almost as if you're trying a bit too hard...'

'I am not!'

Callie instantly denied the accusation. Except that Rowan's words stung hard enough for her to know it was the truth. And hadn't her recent actions shown her how hard she now had to work to dredge up the flirty, party-hearty girl when it had used to be constantly and consistently easy for her?

Maybe she was getting old. Or bored. Or maybe she just needed sex. Or all three.

Rowan traced the pattern of a bold flower on the tablecloth with her finger. 'I read an article the other day about people feeling out of sorts as they approach thirty,' Rowan explained. 'Maybe you're wondering if you're on the right path, whether your life makes sense.'

'Of course my life makes sense,' Callie retorted.

She earned spectacular money doing a job she could do with her eyes closed, she was constantly meeting new people, buzzing from cosmopolitan city to cosmopolitan city. Dinner in Paris…lunch in Rome. Looking at beautiful clothes and making the decisions on what to buy and for whom. She dated cosmopolitan, successful men.

She loved her job. She'd always loved her job. She *still* loved her job…okay, mostly loved her job. She'd been doing it for a long time—she was allowed to feel iffy about it occasionally.

Over the last six months the designers seemed to have become a lot more diva-ish, the cities a bit grimier, the hotel rooms even more soulless than normal. The men more man-scaped than she liked and a great deal more bland.

Maybe she needed a holiday. Or an affair…

'And how's your love-life, Cal? Who's the lucky guy of the moment?'

There Rowan went again—reading her mind. When you'd been friends with someone for more than a quarter of a century it happened. Often.

Callie sipped her wine before answering. 'I'm currently single...'

'You're *always* single,' Rowan corrected her.

'Okay, if you're going to be pedantic then I'll say that I'm currently not sleeping with anyone. Is that better?'

She dated lots of different men and slept with very few of them. Despite her party-girl, flirt-on-two-legs reputation she was very careful who she took into her bed. And she usually found out, during dinner or drinks, that they were married, bi, involved, arrogant or narcissistic. So she normally went to bed alone.

'Marginally. So why aren't you tearing up the sheets with some hunk?' Rowan asked.

Callie twisted her lips. 'Not sure, actually. Nobody has interested me for a while.'

Rowan shoved her tongue into her cheek. 'How long is a while? A week? A month?'

Callie looked at Rowan and tried to ignore the flash of hurt. She knew that Ro was teasing, but saying it like that made her sound like a slut—and she wasn't. She really wasn't. She didn't bed-hop or treat sex casually, but neither was she a nun.

'I haven't slept with anyone for about five, maybe six months,' she admitted quietly.

Rowan instantly looked apologetic. 'Sorry, honey, I didn't mean to sound judgemental. Teasing, maybe— judgy, no.' Rowan waited a beat before speaking again. 'Why not, Cal? You like men and men like you.'

Callie wished she could answer her but she couldn't— not really. Like her avoiding the party scene and her occasional dissatisfaction with her job there was no reason—nothing she could put her finger on. She just hadn't met anyone lately whom she wanted in her bed...in her body. Nobody she liked enough to make the effort.

She just couldn't put her finger on why, and she was

getting a bit tired of her self-imposed celibacy. She liked sex—she needed sex.

'I genuinely don't know, Ro. It just hasn't happened lately and I refuse to force it.' Callie shrugged before sitting up straight and putting a smile of her face. 'Anyway, it's not the end of the world. I'll find someone sooner or later who I'll want to tumble with. In the meantime I have a great, interesting life.'

Rowan bit her lip—a sure sign that she was about to say something that Callie might not like.

'Is it possible that your life is *too* great?'

'Huh? What?' Callie wrinkled her nose, puzzled.

'Your life is so busy, so crazy, and you are so virulently independent—do you have any room in it for a man? A lover? Someone who might be something more than a temporary arrangement? Can it be, darling Cal, that you're too self-sufficient and busy for your own good? Or is it a defence mechanism?'

Okay, had Rowan acquired a psychology degree along with her engagement ring? What was this all about?

'What is *wrong* with you? I came out for a drink—not to be analysed.'

Rowan pulled a face. 'We both had screwed-up childhoods, Cal. My parents and their inability to see me—your mum leaving when you were a little girl. Our push-the-envelope crazy antics got worse and worse the older we got and ended up with you writing off your car when you were eighteen. I landed in jail shortly afterwards.'

'Just for a weekend.'

'That was long enough. That was a hell of year, wasn't it?' Rowan shook her head at the memory.

It had been a hell of a year, indeed, Callie agreed silently.

'After both incidents we...settled down, I suppose.

We're so much better adults than we were kids,' Rowan continued.

'Speak for yourself,' Callie muttered. All she knew for sure was that she'd felt more alive when she was a kid and a wild teenager than she did now. Right now she just felt...*blah*. Not brittle—just *blah*. As if she was a cardboard cut-out of herself.

Rowan sent her a quick, worried look. 'While we're on the subject of your mother, I need to tell you that...'

They were on the subject of *her mother*? Since when? And, oh, hell *no*—they were not going to go there. Not tonight, not tomorrow, not ever. Her mother was long, long gone and not worth wasting time and energy discussing. They most certainly were not on this subject and would never be...

Good try, Ro.

Callie quickly shook her head. 'Don't.'

Rowan held her stare and Callie knew that she was debating whether to get pushy and pursue the topic. Luckily Rowan's mobile rang and she scooped it up off the table. Judging by the soft look on her face, she quickly deduced that it was her brother Seb on the other end, cooing into her ear. She genuinely loved the fact that Seb and Rowan were so unabashedly happy, but their sappiness frequently made her feel queasy.

She couldn't imagine acting like that—being so intertwined, so in tune with another person. It just wasn't her.

Callie looked up when a hand touched her shoulder and saw Jim, the owner of the bar, smiling down at her. He bent to kiss one cheek and then the other, and when he was done she allowed his big fingers to hold her chin.

'Where have you been, hun?'

'Here and there.'

'We've missed you,' Jim stated.

Callie grinned. 'You've missed me starting tequila

shooter competitions which invariably turn into massive parties which lead to your till feeling very full at the end of the evening.'

'That too.' Jim dropped his hand and tipped his head, his expression enquiring. 'Listen, I've got guys at the bar wanting to buy you a drink. You up for company or must I tell them you're not interested?'

Callie didn't bother looking at the bar. She just wanted to talk to Rowan and, if she was lucky, say hi to Finn Banning again. She shook her head. 'I'm not in the mood, Jim—and, besides, I told Rowan that I'd keep a low profile tonight and behave myself.'

'Why do I suspect that that is very difficult for you to do?'

Callie heard the deep, dark voice and whipped her head around to look up and into Finn's face. Tired, she thought, but still oh, so sexy. Purple shadows were painted beneath his eyes and his face looked drawn and thinner. His back and shoulders were taut with tension and his mouth was a slash in his face. She wanted to kiss him and cuddle him at the same time. And she thought that he needed the cuddling a lot more than he needed the kissing.

The last couple of days had clearly put him through the wringer. Experiencing that kind of pain, Callie thought, being that miserable, was why she never got emotionally involved. She'd experienced emotional devastation once before and it wasn't something she ever wanted to deal with again.

However, despite looking like a love refugee, he still looked good. Sage and white striped shirt over faded blue jeans and flat-soled boots. Curls that looked wild from, she guessed, fingers constantly being shoved into them, and a four-day beard. Tough, hard, stoic—and more than a smidgeon miserable.

Yeah, there was that tingle, that bounce in her heart's

step, the womb-clench and the slowly bubbling blood. *This* was what pure attraction—lust—felt like, she remembered. This crazy, want-to-lick-you-silly feeling she'd been missing.

Jim melted away and Finn looked at her with those sexy light eyes. She felt her face flush, her breath hitch.

Sexy, hot, *sad* man. What she wouldn't do to make him smile—she *needed* to make him smile.

'Now, why would you think that?' Callie asked him, projecting as much innocence as she could.

He slapped his hands on his hips and narrowed his eyes at her and she hoped he couldn't tell that her heart was thumping in excitement. He pulled his lips up into a smile which tried but didn't quite make it to his eyes.

'The passage to the bathroom facilities is covered in framed photographs of the parties that have happened here. Not so strangely, you are in most of them—front and centre. Oh, yeah, you're just trouble looking for a place to happen.'

Callie batted her eyelashes at him, her eyes inviting him to laugh with her...at her. 'My daddy told me that talent shouldn't ever be wasted.'

'Your daddy is probably on Prozac.' The smile lifted higher and brushed his eyes.

Progress, she thought.

He shook his head, bemused. 'Trouble. With a capital T. In flashing neon lights.'

Callie left Rowan and Finn discussing the dissolution of all his wedding plans—his eyes had gone back to being flat and miserable, dammit!—and went to sit on a small table on the outside deck, overlooking the harbour. On the mountain behind her lights from the expensive houses twinkled and a cool breeze skittered over the sea, raising goosebumps on her bare arms.

She tucked herself into her favourite corner, out of sight of the bar patrons, and put her feet up on the railing. The sea swished below her feet.

The noise from the bar had increased in volume and, as Finn had observed earlier, usually she'd be in the thick of the action—calling for shots, cranking up the music, and dancing…on the floor, on a bar stool or on the bar itself.

Nobody could ever call her a wallflower, and if they had to then she'd be an exotic one—climbing the wall with her brightly coloured petals and holding a loud hailer.

Where had she gone, that perfect party girl, loud and fearless? She'd cultivated the persona after the car accident—after she'd made a promise to her father and brother to pull herself away from the edge of destruction. It was the only way she'd been able to find the attention she'd craved and she'd got it—especially from men.

She got a lot of attention from men. Apparently it was because, as a previous lover had once told her, men felt good when they were with her: stronger, bolder, more alpha.

Whatever.

But Rowan was wrong. She didn't need a man in her life. Her life was fine—perfect, almost. She had absolutely nothing to complain about. She loved her life, loved her job, the world was her oyster and her pearl and the whole damn treasure chest. She liked her life, liked being alone, being independent, answerable only to herself. Her life was super-shiny. It didn't need additional enhancement.

Besides, as she had learned along the way, to a lot of the men she dated she was a prize to be conquered, a body to possess, a will to be bent. They loved the thrill of the chase and then, because, she didn't do anything but casual, they ended up getting competitive—thought they could be the one to get her to settle down, to commit. That they were 'the man'—had the goods, the bigger set of balls.

They tried to get her to play the role of lover or girl-friend and she always refused. And when their attention became a bit too pointed—when they showed the first signs of jealousy and possessiveness—she backed off. All the way off.

She'd never met a man she couldn't live without, couldn't leave behind. And if she ever had the slightest inkling that she might feel something deeper for someone she was dating she called it quits. She told him that her life was too hectic, too crazy for a relationship, and that wasn't a lie. It just wasn't the whole truth.

She always left before she could be left. It was that simple and that complicated.

Thanks, Mother.

Callie rubbed her forehead with her fingertips, noticing that a headache that was brewing. *Too much thinking, Callie. Maybe you do need a good party after all.*

A brief touch on her shoulder had her jumping and she whirled around. *Finn.* She put her hand on her heart and managed a smile.

'Sorry, I didn't mean to frighten you—you were miles away.' He held a beer bottle loosely in his hand; his other was in the pocket of his jeans. He had a couple of masculine leather and bead bracelets on one wrist and a high-tech watch on the other.

'Hi.' Callie waved him to an empty chair at her table and looked past him into the restaurant. 'Where's Rowan?'

'She met someone she knew at the bar.' Finn yanked the chair out and sat down, stretching his longs legs out in front of him. 'You okay?'

'Shouldn't I be asking that of you?' Callie replied. She leaned forward and asked softly, gently, 'What happened with your fiancée?'

Pain flickered in and out of his eyes. 'You are the nosiest woman I've ever met,' he complained, after taking a long pull of his beer.

'I am—but that doesn't mean I'm not deeply sorry that it happened. Besides, men usually love talking about themselves,' Callie replied.

'Not this one,' Finn replied.

Okay. Back off now, Hollis. Give him some space. 'Can Rowan help you sort out the mess of cancelling the wedding?'

'Luckily, she can. I was just going through the final non-arrangements with her; people are sympathetic but they still need to be paid. Understandable, since pretty much everything that needed to be ordered has already been ordered.'

'I bet Rowan refused to be paid,' Callie said on a small smile. 'She has a heart as big as the sun.'

Finn nodded. 'She did, but she will be—just like everyone else. It's not her fault that things went pear-shaped.'

Pear-shaped? Callie lifted her eyebrows in surprise. Pretty tame word for being jilted. 'So, what happened?' she probed again. Yeah, she was nosy—but this man needed to talk...he needed a friend. Who wouldn't, in his situation? She might be nosy but she could also be a damn good listener.

Finn shook his head. 'I know that you use your eyes as weapons of interrogation, but I'm not going to go there with you.'

Fair enough, Callie thought. He had a right to his secrets. She just hoped that he had someone to talk to—to work this through with.

Finn rolled his head in an effort to release some of the tension in his shoulders. He tapped his index finger against his thigh. 'I *can* tell you that my biggest hassle is that I landed a pretty sweet gig—writing articles about the best honeymoon destinations in Southern Africa. Liz and I were going to spend three weeks travelling…a few days at each destination. My publisher is not going to be happy that I'm doing it solo.'

Callie leaned forward and made a performance of batting her eyelashes. 'Take me—I'll be your substitute wife.'

Finn managed a small grin. 'I'm violently allergic to the word "wife"—even a pretend one.'

'Well, at least you'd be miserable in comfort.'

'If I end up keeping the assignment—which I very well might not.' Finn ran his hands over his short hair and blew out his breath. 'So, tell me why you're sitting here in the dark instead of causing chaos in the bar?'

Callie could clearly see that he'd closed the door on any further discussion about his non-wedding. She looked down into her drink and wrinkled her nose. 'I'm not in the mood to be…'

'Hit on all night?'

'That too. And someone walked in about fifteen minutes ago who I kind of said I might call. We made plans to have supper, then I had to fly to Milan on short notice—'

'Fashion-buying emergency?'

Callie lifted her nose at him in response to his gentle sarcasm. 'Something like that. And I lost his number, and I'm…'

'Not that interested any more?'

She bit her lip. 'Yeah. Not that interested.' She looked out across the ocean to the silver moon that hung low in the sky. She saw the craters, picked out the shape of the rabbit, and sighed.

When she dropped her head her eyes met Finn's and impulsively she reached out and tangled her fingers in his. She ignored the flash of heat, the rocketing attraction. It wasn't the time or the place.

'I'm sorry you're hurting. I'm so sorry for whatever happened that's put such sadness in your eyes.'

Finn licked his lips before staring at the ocean. 'Well, it's not rocket science. I was supposed to be getting married in less than two weeks.'

Callie shook her head, knowing that whatever it was that had mashed up his heart it was more than just losing his ex. 'I think that getting over her will be a lot easier than getting over whatever else has happened.'

Finn's eyes widened and she was surprised when he managed a low, harsh chuckle. He picked at the label on his bottle, not meeting her eyes. 'We changed our minds, decided that marriage wasn't what we wanted—that's all that happened.'

No, it wasn't. But Callie wasn't going to argue with him. 'Well, I am so, so sorry—because it's hurt you badly.'

And for some strange reason the thought of you being hurt makes me feel physically ill.

Finn stood up abruptly and Callie turned to see Rowan approaching them. Finn surprised her when he bent down and kissed her cheek, taking a moment to whisper in her ear.

'Callie, you are part witch and part angel and all sexy. I'm leaving before I say or do anything stupid around you.'

Callie inhaled his aftershave and couldn't help rubbing her cheek against his stubble. 'Like…?'

'Like suggesting that you come home with me.'

His comment wasn't unexpected, and she knew men well enough to know that he was looking for a distraction—a way to step out of the nightmare he was currently experiencing.

Ah, dammit! She wanted to say yes, but she wasn't going to be any man's panacea for pain—even one as sexy as this. If they slept together she wanted it to be because he wanted her beyond all reason and not just to dull the pain, to forget, to step outside his life.

She had to be sensible and she forced the words out. 'Sorry, Finn, that's really not a good idea.'

Finn raked his hand through his hair. 'I know...' He held her eyes and shrugged. 'I really do know. Rowan, hi—I was just leaving...'

CHAPTER TWO

A HALF HOUR LATER Finn tossed down the keys to his house and stared at the coffee-coloured tiles beneath his feet for a moment. Blowing air into his cheeks, he walked through the hall and down the passage to the kitchen, yanked open the double-door fridge and pulled out a beer.

Looking over to the open-plan couch area, he saw the pillow and sheet he'd left on the oatmeal-coloured couch. He'd spent the last few nights on that couch, not sleeping. He couldn't sleep in the bedroom—and not only because he no longer had a mattress on the bed.

Finn rubbed his forehead with the base of the cold bottle, hoping to dispel the permanent headache that had lodged in his brain since last week. Tuesday.

Along with the headache, the same horror film ran on the big screen in his mind...

God, there had been so much blood. As long as he lived he'd remember that bright red puddle on the sheets, Liz grunting beside him, as white as a sheet. He remembered calling for an ambulance and that it had seemed to take for ever to come, remembered Liz sobbing, more blood. The white walls of the hospital, the worried face of the obstetrician. Being told that they had to get Liz into surgery to make sure they didn't lose her too.

It had taken a while for that statement to make sense, and when it had pain had ricocheted through his body and stopped at his heart. Their baby was gone. He also remembered their final conversation as he'd perched on a chair next to her bed, knowing that she was awake but not wanting to talk to him.

'I lost the baby,' she'd said eventually.

'Yeah. I'm so sorry.'

Liz had shrugged, her eyes sunken in her face. 'I feel... empty.' She'd turned her head to look at the flowers he'd bought for her in the hospital gift shop. 'I want to go home, Finn.'

'The doctors say in a day or two. They want to keep an eye on you. You lost a lot of blood. Then I'll take you home.'

Liz shook her head. 'I want to go home—back to Durban, to my folks. We didn't tell anyone I was pregnant so I don't need to explain.'

She fiddled with the tape holding a drip into her vein. When she wouldn't look at him—at all—he knew what she was about to say.

'I don't want to get married any more. We've lost the reason we were both prepared to risk it. We loved the baby but we don't love each other—not enough to get married.'

He rubbed his hands over his face. 'God, Liz. Why don't we take some time to think about that?'

'We don't have time, Finn. And you know that I'm right. If I hadn't fallen pregnant we would've split. You know it and I know it.'

'I'm sorry.'

'Me too.' Liz looked at him then, finally, with pain and sadness and, yes, relief vying for control of her expression. 'Can you cancel the wedding? Sort out the house?'

'Sure.' It was the least he could do.

'And, Finn? I don't want anyone to know that I lost the baby. Just say that we called it quits, okay?'

Now, four days later, he was sad and confused and, to

add hydrochloric acid to an open wound, stuck with all the bills for a wedding that wouldn't happen.

Finn wrestled with the dodgy lock of the door that led out to the balcony and stepped out onto the huge outdoor area. He loved this house—mostly for the tremendous view. From most rooms he had endless views of False Bay, the wildness of the Peninsular, the rocking, rolling Atlantic Ocean. Out here on the balcony he felt he could breathe.

Liz loved the house too, and because she'd spent more time here than he had it seemed as if it was more hers than his. His name might be on the mortgage agreement, but she'd furnished and decorated the place—filled it with the things that made it a home. He supposed that he'd have to go through the place and pack up her stuff—which was pretty much everything. The house would be empty. But to him it felt mostly empty anyway.

They'd tried so hard to play the part of a happy family, but innate honesty had him admitting that, while he was devastated at the loss of their child, he wasn't heartbroken about the wedding being called off. Losing Liz didn't feel like something that had derailed his world, and shouldn't it? Shouldn't he be feeling—*more*? More pain? More confusion? More broken-hearted?

Instead of mourning the loss of his lover he was mourning not being able to hold his child, not being a dad. Although most of his and Liz's conversations lately had revolved around the wedding, they had obviously talked about the birth. They'd been excited—well, *he'd* been excited, Liz had been less so. They'd talked about what type of birth she wanted, had tossed a couple of names around, and he'd been in the process of moving his gym equipment from the third bedroom to the garage so that they could use the room as a nursery.

He felt lousy—as if his world had been tipped upside down. Was it crazy to feel so crap over losing a half-formed, half-baked person to whom he'd contributed DNA but whom he'd never met? Was this normal? Was his grief reasonable? God, he just didn't know.

And how much of his grief was over the baby and how much of it was the residue of the pain he felt about losing James? It felt as if his heart was wrapped in a dull, grey, icy, soggy blanket. The only time he'd felt as if it had lifted—even a little bit—was earlier this evening, when he'd been talking to Callie. For some reason that crazy flirt had managed to lift his spirits. It had been a brief respite and one he'd badly needed.

Finn drank again, leaned his forearms on the railing and stared hard at his feet. He knew that most people thought that because he was a travel journalist that he was a free spirit—that he was a laid-back type of individual—but nothing could be further from the truth. He was a Third Dan black belt in Taekwondo, held a black belt in Jiu-jitsu and, like the other two, his Krav Maga also demanded immense amounts of control and discipline.

But no amount of control, self-discipline or philosophising could rationalise this pain away. Because he'd tried. He really had.

He needed time, he decided—a lot of it—to sort out his head and his heart. Time to think through all he'd recently lost. His baby, his dreams of a family, even his stepdad. He needed time to get back on his feet, to make solid decisions, to work through the emotion of the last couple of weeks, months, years.

And even though he'd been so tempted to ask Callie to come home with him—sleeping with her would have been the perfect way to step out of his head—he knew that he needed to be alone for a while, to keep women at a distance, to work through what had gone wrong with Liz and how.

Ten days, he told himself, and he would be on a plane

to Kruger National Park for the first leg of his Southern Africa trip. Ten days and he could get some distance from this house, from the memory of the blood, Liz's ashen face, from the craziness of cancelling the wedding. Ten days and he would have an excuse to avoid all the calls from his friends and family. He wouldn't have to open the door to any of his three brothers who were taking turns to check up on him, making sure that he was okay.

Finn sighed. Ten more days. A part of him wished he was hiring a kitted-out Land Rover with rooftop tents and heading out into wild, crazy Africa. But visiting upmarket honeymoon destinations wouldn't be a kick in the pants either.

As Callie had said, there was something to be said for licking his wounds in luxury.

If he actually got to keep the job.

The travel magazine had forked out a shedload of cash, and some of the hotels had sponsored his stay in exchange for an honest review of their honeymoon experience. He would be writing the story but he was supposed to take his wife's opinions into consideration as he did so...except now he didn't have a wife to take.

He had to talk to Mike, his editor—and sooner rather than later.

Tomorrow Rowan would send out a blanket email to the wedding guests on his behalf and Mike, as a guest, would receive said email and soon put two and two together. Finn scrunched up his face, annoyed that he hadn't contacted Mike sooner. Cape Town was a small city and he might even have heard already.

Finn glanced at his watch. Ten-thirty. A bit late to call, but that couldn't be helped. He pulled his mobile from his pocket and looked up Mike's number, sighing as he pushed the green button.

'I wondered when you'd get around to calling me,' Mike answered without any preamble.

Finn rubbed his forehead. 'Yeah, it's been a bit mad. I presume you've heard that the wedding is off?'

'Yeah. Sorry.'

Finn heard Mike clearing his throat and jumped in before he could speak again.

'I'd still like to do the assignment.'

'It's a bit pointless without a wife,' Mike said.

'Can't I leave the honeymoon bit out and just write on the lodges themselves?'

'It's scheduled to be part of the honeymoon issue, Finn, with honeymoon and wedding advertising. The article has to concentrate on the honeymoon aspect.'

Finn swore.

Mike's voice in his ear sounded worried and frustrated. 'Tell me about it. I'm in a Catch-22 situation. The publisher agreed to foot the bill, as did many of the hotels, because *you* were writing the article. One of the world's best adventure and travel journalists writing on honeymoons. They loved the idea. And the promo people have already started working on the edition. You're part of that.'

Finn swore again.

'Take me—I'll be your substitute wife.'

He almost smiled, remembering Callie's words from earlier.

Wait, hold on… What had she said?

'Take me—I'll be your substitute wife.'

Could that possibly be a solution? Taking Callie or someone else with him?

'Can I take someone else?' he asked Mike.

Mike's long pause strained Finn's patience. 'I don't see why not,' he said eventually. 'It's not like anyone is going to ask for your wedding certificate or proof that you're married. The two of you would just need to be seen to be having fun. Enjoying the experience. Got anyone in mind?'

He did, actually. Someone who was vivacious, charming, loud, flirtatious, possibly crazy. 'Yeah, I do.'

'Is she someone I know?' Mike asked slyly.

'Judging by the way she talks to everyone and anyone, you probably do.'

'Who is she?'

'Let me talk to her first and see if her coming with me is an option,' Finn said, cautious.

Instinctively he knew that taking Callie—inviting Callie—would be a very good move for him. He'd get to keep this plum assignment and he'd have the company of someone who was a bundle of fun. On that flight back from New York they hadn't stopped talking, and Finn could see why men dropped their tongues to the floor around her. She had a surfer's body—broad shoulders, toned arms, flat stomach and that long, curly blonde hair. But when you looked past the body and face to the brain beyond it you got the shock of your life—because the woman was bright, knowledgeable, and as sharp as a spear-tip.

At her core, she had a lust for life that was contagious. And best of all—unless something had radically changed recently—she had absolutely no interest in relationships and commitment and would be an entertaining companion. She'd be distracting enough to keep him from feeling too sorry for himself.

'Well, talk to her and come back to me. And if you don't take her you'll have to take someone else to complete the assignment,' Mike told him before disconnecting.

Finn slapped his mobile in his hand, considering all his options. He tried to be honest with himself. He had to admit that he was attracted to Callie. If they were spending time in close proximity to each other—he didn't think that honeymoon suites came with twin beds—he'd want

to sleep with her. Hell, he wanted to sleep with her now.
So sue him. His heart might be battered and bruised, but
his junk was in perfectly good working order.

So *sleep with her. It's not like you haven't had flings
before. She could be your rebound girl—your way to get
over and through this bleak time.*

She wouldn't say yes...

How do you know unless you try?

Finn, thinking he might be going off his head, scrolled
through his contacts on his mobile. Rowan would have
her number and after sweet talking her out, he had Callie's mobile number. Taking a deep breath, he pushed the
green phone icon.

'Hey, how do you feel about being my fake wife?'

The next morning Callie rushed around her apartment, trying to get ready. It was crazy that when she was travelling
for work she was super-organised but when she was back
home all her wheels fell off. This morning wasn't the first
time she'd forgotten to set her alarm, and now she was late
for work. So she'd be late? She worked long enough and
hard enough that nobody would make a fuss.

Callie pulled a pale yellow dress over her head and
scrambled in her cupboards for the pair of nude sandals
she wanted to wear with it. Finding them eventually—she
really needed to clean out her overflowing cupboards—
she smiled as she remembered the very odd conversation
she'd had with Finn last night about being his fake wife.

She'd always thought that the 'wife for hire' premise in
romance novels was odd, because she couldn't conceive
of a situation in the twenty-first century when a fake wife
would ever be needed.

But gorgeous Finn needed a wife. She was sorry that she
couldn't help him out, but thanks to the eye-watering mortgage she paid each month on this flat, her job—even when

she wasn't crazy about it—always came first. Which was a shame, because she could totally see herself swanning around five-star resorts, drinking cocktails and snuggling up to her husband's hot bod—fake...real...who cared?

With her hair and make-up done, Callie headed to the kitchen. She pulled open her fridge door with more hope than expectation and twisted her lips at the bare shelves. There was absolutely nothing to eat and she was starving.

But she knew of a house where there would be blueberry muffins and a hot pot of coffee. The downside was that she'd be even later for work than normal, but maybe she'd take the morning off, or even the day. The house was only a couple of minutes away, and a large part of the reason why she'd bought this expensive flat in this gated community.

Awelfor, red-bricked and old, was her childhood home. In it were her favourite people; Seb, her brother, her best friend and almost sister-in-law Rowan, and Yasmeen, their housekeeper.

But she was so much more than a housekeeper, Callie thought ten minutes later, when she stood in the big, bright sunny kitchen at Awelfor, bending over to hug Yasmeen. This tiny, fiery Malay woman was her north star, her homing beacon. Awelfor would not be home without her.

Yasmeen pulled away and lifted her hand to Callie's face. Her black eyes narrowed. 'You're too skinny and you look tired. When are you going to spend more time on land than you do in the air? And when are you going to find a man and have some babies?'

Situation normal, Callie thought. It was fine for Yasmeen to be a spinster, but not her. *Do as I say and not as I do* was Yas's position on this subject.

Callie rolled her eyes and snagged a muffin—choc chip, not blueberry, yum!—from the plate in the middle of the wooden table that dominated the kitchen.

'Don't nag me—nag them,' Callie retorted, gesturing to Seb and Rowan who had walked into the kitchen, both of them wearing that just-had-spectacular-wake-up-sex look.

Lucky rats. Callie wrinkled her nose when Finn's gorgeous face flashed onto her eyeballs. She'd love to wake up to morning sex with *him*.

Seb crossed the kitchen to where she perched on the corner of the table, munching her muffin. As usual, he kissed her temple and gave her a quick hug. Her brilliant, nice brother. She was so happy that he'd found Ro—that they'd found each other.

It almost, but not quite, made her believe in true love. If it existed then Seb and Ro had the best chance of experiencing it.

Callie was startled out of her musings by Yasmeen's hand slapping her thigh. She yelped and looked at her accusingly. 'What?' she demanded.

'Have you *ever* been allowed to sit on the table instead of at it?' Yasmeen demanded, hands on her hips. 'That's what chairs are for.'

Callie pulled a face at Rowan, who was laughing at her, but jumped off the table and pulled a chair out to sit down. 'Yas...?' she wheedled, using her best little-girl voice.

'Yes, I know—you want a stuffed omelette,' Yasmeen replied, heading to the fridge.

'You know me so well,' Callie purred.

'I should. You've had me wrapped around your little finger since you were a baby,' Yas retorted, pulling items out of the fridge. 'Make yourself useful and grate some cheese.'

Seb poured them all some coffee and placed a cup on the table in front of Callie. 'Aren't you late for work?' he asked, glancing at his watch.

Callie shrugged. 'I let them know. Besides, I have so

much holiday time due to me that I can take a morning here and there.'

She unwrapped the cheese and placed it on the cutting board Yasmeen had placed in front of her. Yasmeen passed her a grater and Callie got to work.

'Hey, Ro?'

'Mmm?' Rowan looked up from her job of cutting red bell peppers. In Yas's kitchen everyone helped. Including Seb, who was dicing mushrooms.

'I had a call from the sexy Finn last night.'

'What sexy Finn?' Seb demanded. 'Is this another European man you're dating?'

Callie laughed. 'No, this is Ro's client Finn. The one we went to meet last night.'

Callie pinched some cheese and popped it into her mouth. After chewing, she told them about Finn's crazy be-my-fake-wife offer.

Rowan looked at her, bemused. 'Are you mad? Take him up on it!'

'I'm flying to Paris, Ro, I have a job.'

'You've just said that you have so much holiday time owed to you,' Ro argued.

'Stop encouraging her to act crazy, darling,' Seb told Rowan. 'And running off with a man she doesn't know would be crazy. Talking about crazy—Cal, we need to talk.'

The mood in the room instantly turned serious as Seb cleared his throat. Rowan frowned and bit her bottom lip. Yasmeen stopped beating the eggs and Seb stared down at his pile of fungi.

Something was up, and whatever it was she knew from their response that she wouldn't like it. 'What's going on?' she asked.

Seb sent Rowan a pleading look, but Rowan just shook her head. Seb looked at her, fear and worry and, strangely, a touch of excitement in his deep blue eyes. 'Cal, I have to tell you something.'

Callie shook her head, knowing instinctively that she didn't want to hear whatever he was going to say. She held up her hand. 'I don't want to know.'

'Laura is coming home.'

Crap. Dammit. Hell.

Laura. Her mother. *Their* mother. The woman, as Seb had told her a few months back, he had reconnected with. Oh, she'd always suspected that he'd kept track of her; he was a brilliant ethical hacker and there wasn't any information he couldn't find.

'I want to see her again and she's returning to Cape Town for a visit.'

Seb had a stubborn look on his face and she knew that his mind was made up.

'Are you paying for her to come home?' Callie demanded.

Seb's lack of an answer was confirmation that he was.

'If you bring her back to Awelfor I'll never forgive you,' Callie whispered, her stomach now in a knot, twisted with tension and long-ago suppressed hurt.

Her mother had walked out when she was seven. As far as Callie was concerned she'd had twenty years to come back home. It was way too late now.

'I wasn't planning to—not yet,' Seb said in a quiet voice. 'She's coming home for a three-week visit and we've agreed to meet. She wants to see you too.'

Callie shook her head wildly. 'Hell, no! No to the max. *No!*'

Seb held up his hands. 'I know that this is a shock, but...'

Callie pulled in a deep breath and pushed back the hurt, the feeling of abandonment, the constant ache for her mother. Her eyes turned cold and her face tightened.

'When is she due to land?' she asked quietly, thinking that this was what Rowan had started to tell her the other night. She had been trying to warn her about Laura's arrival—trying to get her head wrapped around the idea of Laura returning.

Sorry, Ro, not even marginally interested.

Seb checked his watch. 'Today is the eleventh; she's flying in on the nineteenth. Will you be back in town by then?'

Callie grabbed her mobile from her bag and quickly pulled up her diary app. She cursed when she saw that after Paris she didn't have any trips scheduled for a couple of weeks. Three, to be exact. It was the end of a three-month rotation—but why, oh, why did it have to be now?

She'd be home at exactly the same time as her mother would be in the city. That wouldn't do. That wouldn't do at all. She wouldn't risk running into her, having her arrive on her doorstep, popping into Awelfor and seeing her here. She wouldn't take the chance.

She'd endured twenty years of silence and Laura didn't just get to rock up now and make demands. She'd made her choice when she left—she had to live with it now.

'Will you try to be here?' Seb asked quietly, rephrasing his question.

Callie shook her head before yanking her bag off the chair and heading for the door. 'Hell, no. I don't have a mother—I haven't had one for twenty years. So Laura can just go back to wherever she came from and I don't want to talk about her again. *Ever!*'

'Cal—' Seb pleaded.

'Don't mention her name again, Seb,' Callie muttered, before stepping out of the door, blinking back tears. It had to be the bright sunlight making her cry because her mother—*Laura!*—wasn't worth a single one of her tears.

Looking down at her mobile in her hand, she thought

that she couldn't be in the country, breathing the same air as Laura. She'd rather do anything else, *be* anywhere else. Even—

'Finn? It's Callie. You called me last night? If you haven't married, proposed to or found anybody else to be your wife since we spoke last night I might be your girl.'

CHAPTER THREE

CALLIE LEFT AWELFOR and headed directly to Simon's Town, the pretty town to the east of the city of Cape Town. Her father had set up a branch of his sea kayaking tours there after handing over the family property business to Seb. Patch loved his life as a kayak guide and tour operator. Like her, he was vivacious and open; if she had any charm at all she'd inherited it all from him.

Callie sat on the low wall that separated the promenade from the beach and watched Patch converse with his customers while his assistants unloaded the kayaks from the trailer that he'd driven onto the beach. He was still tall and broad and handsome—quite a silver fox, Callie thought. Thank God he'd finally given up dating vapid and beautiful women—mostly younger than her—and was about to marry a woman his own age.

He and Annie seemed to be blissfully happy, and after what Laura and the crazy gold-diggers had put him through she was happy for him. He deserved to be loved and loved well. And, judging by the perpetual grin he was sporting lately, Annie loved him very well indeed.

Callie let out a whistle that Patch had taught her as a kid and Patch instantly turned, his fantastic smile lighting up his face. She might have had a screwed-up childhood, and maybe Patch hadn't been the perfect father, but it had been a very long time since she'd doubted that he loved her. He was one of her best friends and the strongest rope keeping the balloon that was her life tethered to the ground.

Patch bounded across the sand and immediately pulled her into his arms, warm and strong. She buried her head in his neck, sucked in the smell of him and felt her tilting world settle down. Patch ran a hand over her hair before kissing her temple and stepping away from her to sit on the wall next to her.

'Seb told you, huh?'

'Yeah.' She suddenly remembered that her mother had been his wife and wondered how *he* was handling the news. 'How do you feel about her returning?'

Patch shrugged. 'Doesn't mean much to me except for how it affects you and Seb.'

Callie sank her bare feet into the warm sand and wiggled her toes. She bit the side of her lip and stared out to sea. 'I'm running away...'

Patch cocked his head. 'You are? Where to?'

'Well, it's not quite settled, but there's this guy and he needs a—a friend to go on a trip with him.'

'Uh-huh?'

'He seems nice, and he's just gone through a rough time, and we seem to like each other...' Callie waved her hands in the air. 'Not as...you know...but I think we could be friends... He needs a friend.'

'Most of us do,' Patch agreed. 'And you want to avoid seeing Laura.'

Callie waited a beat before turning anxious eyes to his face. 'Am I wrong? Should I be meeting her?'

Patch ran his hand over his jaw. 'Honey, for the last ten years, ever since you totalled your car at a thousand miles an hour, I have trusted you to do the right thing—not for me but for yourself. I still trust you to do that.' He reached for her hand and held it. 'That thing we call intuition? That little voice? It's your soul talking. You can trust it.'

'My intuition is telling me to go on this trip with Finn.'

'Then do it,' Patch said, before frowning. 'Wait—is this Rowan's client? The travel writer?'

'Mmm.'

Patch smiled broadly. 'Tell him to come kayaking with me—maybe he'll do an article on the tours.'

Callie had to smile. Her dad was her rock, but he was never shy about putting himself forward. Ah, well, she thought as she sat with him in the morning sun, you don't get apples from orange trees.

Callie buzzed Finn through the gates of her complex in Camps Bay and walked onto the wide veranda that encompassed most of her second-storey luxury flat. She leaned her arms on the railing, watching as he steered his expensive SUV into her visitor's parking space. He left his vehicle and Callie watched as he stretched, his T-shirt riding up his abdomen to reveal a ridged stomach that had to be an eight or ten-pack and the hint of make-women-stupid obliques.

She did appreciate a fine-looking man, Callie thought, and they didn't come much finer than Finn Banning. Sexy, and also very successful She'd researched him and read that he had been an award-winning investigative journalist before switching to travel journalism, where he was raking in the praise.

What had really gone wrong with his engagement? Why had they called it off? Why would any woman walk away from that?

Maybe there was something about Finn Banning that she didn't know yet—and that worried her. Especially if she was considering spending three weeks in his company.

After she'd called him from Awelfor she'd spent ten minutes convincing him that she wasn't joking about being his 'wife' and avoiding his probing questions around why she'd changed her mind. She'd ended the conversation with the suggestion that if he still thought that taking her along was a good idea he should pop by for a drink at sunset.

And here he was—still hot, still sexy, still sad and still, apparently, wifeless.

He was her get-out-of-the-country card. Okay, the truth was that she didn't need him to go anywhere—she had enough cash at her disposal to go anywhere she wanted. But since she was taking a month's holiday at very short notice wherever she went she would be going alone. Normally she wouldn't mind being alone, but at the moment she needed a distraction from her thoughts—from thinking about Laura.

She'd thought she'd buried those feelings of betrayal and abandonment but apparently it only took the knowledge that Laura was heading home to pull them all back up to the surface.

If she went anywhere alone she'd think and wallow and feel sad and miserable. But if she went with Finn she'd have a sexy man to distract her; she'd have to be happy and flirty and...well, *herself.*

She could shove all thoughts of Laura back into the box they'd escaped from.

Finn pulled off his sporty sunglasses and held them in his hand as he looked around the complex, eventually seeing her number on the front wall. He rubbed the back of his neck as he stopped a couple of feet from her door—a gesture that told Callie he wasn't totally comfortable with this idea and was thinking of backing out.

'Finn...hi.' She leaned over the balcony to look down at him, not aware that she was giving him a super-excellent view of her hot pink lace-covered breasts. 'The door is open. Come on up the stairs and hang a left. It's too gorgeous an evening to be inside.'

Finn nodded and walked through the front door. She

heard the thud of the door closing behind him, and his rapid footsteps told her that he was jogging up the stairs. Through the wooden patio doors she saw him entering her lounge, looking around at the eclectic furniture and her wild, colourful abstract art. He dropped his glasses, mobile and keys on her coffee table and looked at her across the room.

His eyes caught hers and a small smile played on his lips. 'Hello, possible fake wife.'

Callie laughed, immediately at ease. What was it about him that instantly had her relaxing? She felt she'd known him a lot longer than she had.

She watched as Finn stopped, as everyone always did, at the wall of photo frames. She watched his eyes skim over the photographs, quickly taking in her history—her journey from being a daredevil kid to a daredevil teenager to who she was today, whoever *that* was.

Finn spent more time than people usually did staring at the photos, eventually turning to look at her, his eyebrows raised. 'You're up a tree.'

'I frequently was.'

He pointed to a frame. 'You look like you're about forty feet up.'

She grinned. 'Forty-two feet—my dad measured it after his heart restarted.' She shrugged and waved her wine glass around. 'They told me not to climb it, so I did.'

'How old were you?'

'Five? Six? Somewhere around there.'

'You must have been a handful.'

'You have no idea. I thought I was indestructible. I had zero sense of self-preservation and was willing to try anything once—or four times. And if my brother was giving something a whirl—well, I would too. Surfing, diving, climbing, skateboarding, cycling...'

'And I thought *I* was a hellraiser. Your mum must have pulled her hair out,' Finn said, walking towards her.

Callie swallowed and looked away. Her mum had let her run wild—not particularly worried that Callie might crack her head open or break a limb. She would just shake her head before disappearing into her bedroom and locking the door behind her.

Then one day, a couple of weeks after her seventh birthday, she'd disappeared for ever.

Finn stepped out onto the veranda, gratefully taking the beer she held out to him. She dropped into the corner of her fat couch and tucked her bare feet up and under her bottom, gesturing to Finn to take a seat. When he'd sat down in the chair next to her he looked out at the sea view and the dropping sun and sighed.

'Nice place. How long have you lived here?'

'I bought it about five years ago. I love it, but I'm seldom home,' Callie explained, picking up her wine glass and taking a sip. She turned and looked at his profile, strong in the fading light of the day.

'So what's happened that you're suddenly available to come travelling?' Finn asked. 'And why are your eyes red-rimmed and puffy?'

Damn, that cosmetics rep had *so* lied. The eye cream that had cost the equivalent of a small house did *not* suck away the bags of fluid left there by a massive crying jag.

Callie couldn't meet his eyes. Mostly because she felt her own prickling with tears again and she never cried in company—especially not around sexy, fit men. 'It's not important.'

Finn shook his head. 'I suspect it's very damn important to you.' Then he lifted one broad shoulder. 'But, since I hate people prying, I'll leave you with your secrets.'

Thank you, she thought sarcastically, a little put out that he hadn't pushed. Did that mean that she actually *wanted* to tell him her sad tale of maternal neglect? *Blergh*—she didn't do sob stories. Especially her own.

Callie pulled herself out of her funk and tilted her head. 'So, it turns out that I can be free for the next four weeks or so. Do you want to explain your crazy proposal to me again?'

Finn stretched out his long legs, which ended in a pair of battered trainers. 'As I explained, I landed an assignment to write an article on upmarket lodges, focusing on the honeymoon aspect of said lodges. The magazine is Europe-based, a leader in its field, it has a huge readership and it's a plum assignment.'

'Of course it is.'

Finn was hot property—he wouldn't be writing for just any old magazine.

'With the wedding imploding I either have to give up the assignment or find someone to go with me.'

'As your wife?'

'As my editor said, nobody is going to ask for proof of my marriage. If I take someone who looks reasonably happy to be there with me I think I can get by without having to explain that the wedding was called off two weeks before the big day,' Finn said, his voice even but his expression pensive. 'I really don't want to give up the opportunity to get my foot in the door with *Go Travel*; they have a bunch of staff writers and rarely issue assignments to freelancers.'

But they did to you.

As she'd thought: hot property, indeed. And not just as a writer. The man had a body that you could strike tinder off.

Callie resisted the urge to fan her face with her hand as a bead of sweat trickled down her spine. Yes, it was summer in Cape Town, but her hot flush had nothing to do with the evening heat and everything to do with imagining him naked above her, his fabulous eyes locked on hers as he pushed himself home. She'd be tight and he'd be big, and he'd reach that special spot deep inside and rock her to screaming...

'Callie?'

Finn's voice pulled her out of her side trip into fantasy land and she waved a hand in front of her face, knowing that her cheeks were fire-red. 'Wow, it's so hot out here.'

'Actually, a cool breeze has picked up and the temperature has dropped a couple of degrees,' Finn countered, sending her a knowing smile. At least she thought it was knowing—for all she knew he could be thinking that she was loopy.

She fumbled for her wine and downed half a glass before resting it on her cheek.

'You okay?'

Just peachy, trying to deal with the fact that you are the first man I can imagine sleeping with for far too long.

'Fine.'

Liar, liar, womb on fire....

'Anyway, back to your trip. When are you supposed to arrive at your first destination? Where *is* the first destination?'

'The Baobab and Buffalo Lodge, which is on a private concession next to the Kruger National Park. We're booked in for a few nights.'

Holy fishcakes—when they said 'upmarket' they meant *upmarket*. Callie knew that the Baobab and Buffalo Lodge was booked solidly for years at a time. It was a six-star safari experience all the way.

Callie leaned forward, her eyes uncharacteristically serious. 'Cards on the table, Finn. What exactly does it entail? What do you expect from me?'

A ghost of a smile flitted over Finn's face. 'All it entails is you hanging out at expensive lodges and hotels, taking part in some of the activities, eating yourself into a coma and drinking yourself under the table. All on my expense account.'

'And the cons?'

'You have to do all of that with me.' Finn placed his ankle on his knee and picked at the label of his beer bottle. 'I'd like someone I can talk to—someone I could have fun with…someone who I know is not going to go all hearts and flowers on me, thinking that this will be the start of something special. I am in no way, shape or form looking to extend this beyond the holiday, nor looking for anything more than a friendship.'

Okay, she could understand that. Everybody needed time to regroup after a break-up, and of course he didn't want to get involved. And she was perfect for that as she didn't go hearts and flowers on any man, ever. And she was fun.

Well, she hadn't been fun for a while, but that was going to change. She'd pull herself out of her funk and go back to being the old, crazy, happy, party-like Callie.

She needed to be that Callie again.

Callie cocked her head. Time to pull out the big guns. 'And this *fun*. Where does it stop? In other words, are you expecting sex out of this deal?'

Finn's light eyes bumped into hers. 'It would be a nice side benefit but not a deal-breaker.'

Callie heard the honesty in his words and tone but thought she should just make sure. 'So I could still go with you and not be pressurised into having sex with you?'

Honesty had her silently admitting that she probably would—old Callie wouldn't have hesitated!—but she'd prefer to have it out in the open.

'Making me repeat it in another way isn't going to make my words more true. But if it makes you happy…' Finn lifted that broad shoulder again. 'Sex—if it happens—

will be a bonus, not an expectation. And totally without strings.'

Callie nibbled the inside of her lip, desperately trying to be sensible. She couldn't believe that she was seriously considering his offer, but on the other hand how often did the opportunity to visit such wonderful places in luxury— for free!—fall into one's lap?

How often did a person get the chance to do something so different on someone else's dime? That would be *never*. She'd be a fool to pass this up.

But she wasn't an idiot. She had to be marginally sensible about this. She was thinking about going on holiday with a stranger—a man she'd met twice. If he turned out to be a psycho she would be at his mercy, neck-deep in a situation that might become very sticky, very fast.

But he didn't give off any creepy vibes, and she had pretty good intuition. *It's your soul talking...you can trust it.* She suspected he was exactly what he appeared to be: a guy who'd had the emotional carpet yanked from underneath his feet; battered, who was bruised and trying to find his feet, to regroup.

But was she prepared to risk her life on her intuition?

'I'll need character references.' she blurted out, hoping that he would understand that she needed to protect herself. 'Just to make sure that you aren't a weird psycho. I can give you references too, if you want.'

At that, Finn did smile—possibly the fullest and most genuine smile she'd yet to see from him. 'Nah, I'm good. I already know that you're slightly psycho,' he teased.

'Funny...' Callie muttered, although in truth he was. It was a relief to realise that behind that gruff, stoic exterior was an offbeat sense of humour. When you travelled with someone a GSOH was the minimum requirement.

Callie put down her glass of wine and linked her fingers around her bare knee. 'Are you sure about this, Finn?

You don't know me. After two days with me, you might want to shoot me.'

Finn lifted the beer bottle to his lips, took a long sip and swallowed. 'If we were at a resort and I had to say to you that I wanted some time alone, some quiet, what would you do?'

Callie thought for moment. 'I'd find something to do— go hang out by the pool, read my book, flirt with the barman. I'd give you your space.'

'And if I said let's go bungee jumping or white-water rafting?'

'I'd say go on your own,' Callie replied quickly. She held up her hand and looked at him askance. 'Is me being a thrill-seeker part of the requirement? Because if it is then I might have to bail now. You might be Indiana Jones, but I'm not a run-through-the-jungle-barefoot type of girl.'

She had been at one time. Right up until her late teens— until her car accident—she'd tried anything wild or woolly once...probably twice.

Finn's mouth twitched with amusement as he glanced towards the photos on the wall before looking back at her. 'Fair enough. You might change your mind.'

No, she wouldn't. He could take that to the bank.

'You have a better chance of falling pregnant,' Callie quipped before turning serious again. 'Look, Finn, I'm honoured and flattered that you've asked me to go with you, but this will only work if you feel you can be honest with me, that you can treat me like you were taking a mate with you.' Her brows pulled together. 'Why *aren't* you taking a friend with you? Surely you have someone you could ask?'

'You keep forgetting the honeymoon angle.' Finn pushed his hand through his short curls. 'The magazine is paying through the nose for me to do this, and there is no way they will allow me to go on my own or with a mate.

They were expecting me to go with my wife, at the very least my girlfriend, at the very, *very* least with a woman.' Finn placed his beer on the wooden coffee table between them. 'So what do you think? Yes? No? Hell, no?' Finn raised a solid black eyebrow.

Callie nodded. 'I think so.' She slowly answered him. 'Let me have a bit more of a think.'

Why was she hesitating, being coy about this? She wanted, *needed*, to get out of Cape Town, and Finn was offering her a brilliant way to do that. She found him easy to talk to, he seemed to like her, and she was attracted to him.

What was holding her back?

Exactly that, she realised. The fact that she was so immensely attracted to him. Nobody had ever created such an intense longing in her and that made her wary...a little scared. If she were less drawn to him she wouldn't have any doubts and she'd be packing her bags already.

You are so weird, Hollis, Callie told herself. *Fruitcake nuts.*

'I'd love to know what is going through that very sharp brain of yours, Callie.'

There was no chance of her telling him what she was thinking. *I know that you were about to be married, and that you're probably hurting and missing your fiancée, but I'd really like to have you leaning over me, sliding on home...*

She didn't think so.

On the other hand she really didn't want to be someone's backstop. If Finn was making love to her then she wanted him to be *with* her, thinking of her and not of the lover he'd lost. She wasn't prepared to be his escape, his emotional aspirin, a distraction from the pain. She'd be his friend, but if he made love to her then it would be because he wanted her.

While she was prepared to be a fake wife, she refused

to be a second choice or a substitute lover. Maybe if she knew why he was so suddenly single she would have a better idea of how emotionally battered he really was. And the only way to get that information was to ask.

'Why *did* your engagement blow up?'

Finn glared at her. 'You are like a dog with a freakin' bone. Do you ever give up?'

Innate honesty compelled her to speak. 'No.'

Callie stared at him with big eyes as he stood up, walked around the table and gripped the arms of her chair, caging her in. Callie sucked in air and along with it the masculine, indefinable essence of Finn. A kick of spice, a hint of citrus, a tiny bit of natural musk. The hair on her arms and on the back of her neck stood up and she felt her skin prickle as his eyes locked on hers.

'Are you always this stubborn?'

Callie shook her head. 'Sorry to tell you that I haven't even hit stubborn yet.'

'Crap. Well, let's see if a little distraction will work,' Finn replied, his voice silky. 'And if my kisses don't distract you at least they'll get you to shut the hell up...'

Callie sucked in her breath as his mouth brushed her lips. Harder, thinner, masculine lips that knew exactly what they were doing as he nipped and teased her mouth. His hand came up to clasp the side of her head and he tipped her face sideways. Then his kiss deepened and his mouth became more insistent, asking—no, *demanding*—more.

'Kiss me, Callie. Open up and let me taste you,' he muttered against her lips.

Callie couldn't do anything but obey—didn't have the thought processes to do anything but follow where he led.

Instead of plunging inside, forcing its way in, his smart tongue explored her bottom lip, teased the corners of her mouth, deliberately avoided tangling with hers.

Frustrated with his teasing, Callie pushed against his

chest and, keeping her mouth locked on his, found her way to her feet, looping her arms around his back and pushing into his hard frame. Breast against chest, stomach against his steel erection, mouth under his. Needing more, she pushed her tongue into his mouth, sliding it against his and taking the kiss from hot to steamy to erotic, from wild to crazy.

His hands raced down her back, palmed her butt and lifted her up and into him. Her legs automatically wound around him and she tipped her hips so that his erection could rub her clit as his kisses—God, was it possible?—got deeper and steamier.

She wanted more...she needed more... This was just sex, lust! Six months was far too damn long, Callie realised from a place way, way outside of herself. She needed him—Finn—now.

Her hands were sliding down the back of his shorts, trying to feel that magnificent ass she'd been fantasising about, when Finn pulled his mouth off hers. He lifted his hand from the inside of her bra and one arm kept her anchored in place. He brushed her hair off her cheek and tucked it behind her ears. He looked rueful.

Callie felt her feet touch the floor and she held on to his arm to make sure that she wouldn't topple over.

'Ah...um...what was that?'

'God knows. But, after that I guess sex is closer to being on the table than before.'

Finn stepped away from her, seemingly unconcerned that he still had a steel pipe in his pants.

His words dumped a figurative bucket of cold water over her head. What *was* it about him? He just had to touch her and she was under his spell, ready to go where he led. She never lost control in a sexual situation—her head was always in the game.

'That's why I'm wary,' Callie admitted eventually, unable to stop licking her bottom lip, hoping the taste of him lingered there.

Finn's black brows pulled together. 'Sorry—lost you. What?'

'We have a hectic attraction. It could blow up in our faces,' Callie explained. 'It could burn hot and die fast, and if that happens while we're on holiday then we'd be up the creek without a paddle.'

Finn jammed his hands in the pockets of his shorts. 'We'll be together for three weeks. Do you normally lose interest that quickly?'

Sometimes, Callie wanted to admit. But with him she was more worried about feeling something deeper than basic lust than finding herself bored. Bored, she could fake her way through, but he intrigued her; he was a puzzle she longed to solve and that rarely...okay, *never* happened to her. And if she was this attracted to him—physically and mentally—so soon, then spending twenty-four-seven with him might make her feel so much more.

Dangerous.

Callie stepped away and held up her palms. *Okay, get a grip and shut this down before it goes any further. Get you head in the game, Hollis. Someone has to be sensible here and it looks like you've drawn the short straw.*

'Finn, I get that you're hurting, that you need a distraction from your crappy life. You've just broken up with your fiancée and that's got to be seriously painful.'

And I'm using you to escape dealing with my mother.

Finn just folded his arms and kept his face blank.

'You should know that I never treat sex casually, that I am very selective about who I bring into my bed.'

'Okay. Good to know.'

Callie blew out her breath. 'And you should also know that I'm not going to be your means of escaping that pain.'

And, conversely, I'm not going to use you to escape my memories.

Finn frowned. 'Lost you. Explain.'

She waved her hand in the space between them. 'We obviously generate some heat between us, and I have no doubt that sleeping with you would be fun, but we can't ignore the fact that until recently you were in a highly committed relationship. That relationship came to a skidding halt and pretty much went over a cliff. Fair to say that?'

Finn shrugged. 'I suppose.'

'So, to carry on with that analogy, I'm not going to sleep with you until I am fully convinced that you have come out of that coma and are mostly recovered. I'm *not* a way to dull the pain.'

Finn stared at her for a long time, his green eyes speculative. Eventually, ever so slightly, his mouth lifted at the corners. 'This isn't all about me and my relationship, is it? You're also running from something—or *someone*.'

Maybe. Possibly. Okay, dammit, yes.

'And that's why you've been crying.' Finn rubbed his jaw with the palm of his hand. After a long silence he lifted his muscled shoulders in a weary shrug. 'Look, Callie, I'm probably not ever going to tell you about the mess that was my almost-marriage, but would you think I was spinning a line to get into your pants if I said that I'm not that heartbroken? That I'm sad but also relieved?'

She heard something that sounded like the ring of truth in his voice but she didn't know him well enough to trust him. 'Maybe you're just telling yourself that to make it easier to cope with. People love to lie to themselves.' She saw Finn's mouth open to start his protest but she shook her head to stop him. 'Look, Finn, let's just take it slow, okay? One day at a time, as friends and companions. Let's not force it, okay?'

He looked as if he wanted to argue, but then she saw him swallowing his words, saw his nod.

'Yeah, okay, I suppose that's sensible.'

Finn lifted his hand to brush her cheek with the backs of his fingers. Callie could only look at him, her blood roaring through her veins and pooling between her legs. If he didn't go soon she was going to forget any doubts she had and drag him to the floor.

'That being said, I'm going to go.'

Callie licked her lips as her brain tried to restart. 'Um... okay.' Him going would be a very good idea.

'You'll let me know your decision? As soon as possible? Like tomorrow?'

Callie handed him a blank look. 'Uh...what decision?'

Finn grinned. 'About being my fake wife?'

Callie blushed. God, her brains were fried. 'Sure, as soon as possible.'

She opened her mouth to add a blanket yes to whatever he wanted, wherever he wanted, as long as he would kiss her like that again. At the last minute her rationality kicked in and mentally slapped her to bring her to her senses.

'I'll see you out.'

'Don't bother.'

Finn stepped towards her, dropped a quick kiss on her temple before heading inside and picking up his wallet, keys and mobile. He turned and looked at her, and the corner of his mouth kicked up.

'Yeah, I think you and I could have some fun. And, Cal?'

'Mmm?'

'No more crying, okay?'

CHAPTER FOUR

FINN HEARD HIS doorbell ring and cursed as he lifted another box onto the tower of boxes he was creating in his hallway. God, Liz had a lot of stuff, he thought as he turned sideways to navigate through the thin aisle between boxes to get to the door.

It would be a brother again, holding a six-pack and a takeaway, coming to keep him company in his darkest hour. He appreciated the beer and the food, but instead of their sympathy he wished that they'd give him something useful, like help with shifting and packing boxes.

He rolled his eyes as the doorbell pealed again and reached out to yank the door open. 'You can only come in if you're prepared to work, you lazy—'

He blinked at the vision on his doorstep. Instead of one of his big, brawny, young stepbrothers Callie, dressed in a short sleeveless sundress, stood in front of him, her blonde hair pulled up into a tail and most of her face covered by huge dark sunglasses.

'Oh, sorry. Wasn't expecting you.'

Callie pushed her glasses up into her hair and smiled. 'I can see that, since you're shirtless and shoeless. Who *were* you expecting?'

'Ah, one or more of my brothers—stepbrothers. They pop in most evenings, usually around this time.'

'Coming to check up on you?'

'Yeah.'

Callie placed a hand on her heart. 'That's so sweet.'

Finn grimaced. 'I appreciate the sentiment but I wish they would just stop. Because I'm not talking they think that Liz is to blame and that I need comforting.'

'*Is* she to blame?'

'Mutual decision,' he replied quickly, seeing the trap and dodging it. 'Anyway, because not all men are Neanderthals, they've been worried about me because Liz and I were together for a long time. I have so many offers for beer or lunch or dinner I could scream.'

Callie didn't say anything and he, like a rookie, just kept on talking.

'So I drink the beers and eat the food and try to convince everyone that I'm okay.'

'Are you?'

Callie took his right hand and held it between hers. She looked up at him from beneath those ridiculously long lashes, her expression earnest and concerned. She wasn't just asking for form's sake, he suddenly realised, she genuinely seemed to care. And her empathy—not pity or sympathy—melted one of the many icicles attached to his heart.

Finn thought about her question for a minute and left his hand where it was, his fingers entangled with hers. 'Mostly. I will be a feeling a lot more relieved when you say yay or nay.'

'Yay,' Callie said as she dropped his hand.

Finn looked down at her, not sure that he'd heard her correctly. 'What?'

'Yes, I will be your fake wife.' Callie said, her eyes dancing. 'Thanks for asking me.'

Finn felt relief course through him and was surprised at the wave of—hell—*happiness* that followed. He was going to be able to complete this amazing assignment, get out of this house and step out of his life, thanks to this phenomenal woman.

'That's the best news I've heard all day. Thanks, Callie.'

'I should be thanking you; it's an amazing opportunity to see some places that I haven't seen before.'

'And to get out of Dodge as well.' Finn folded his arms and raised a brow. 'Want to tell me why?'

Callie didn't miss a beat. 'Want to tell me what really happened to stop the wedding?'

'Touché.'

He wasn't going to open up and neither was she. Better that way, Finn decided, even though he was damn curious.

'So, do you want to come inside?'

Finn thought that she was about to say no but then she straightened her spine and pushed her shoulders back, lifting those small breasts. 'Yeah, okay. There's a couple of things we need to chat about.'

'That sounds ominous.' Finn gestured her inside and noticed that she had no problem negotiating the boxes. 'Liz's stuff. I'm packing it up and shipping it home to her parents.'

'Ah.'

Callie moved away from the boxes and looked at the now stark living room. All the things that had made it a home were gone—the scatter cushions, the art, the ornaments, the photo frames.

'The furniture—hers or yours?'

Finn shrugged. 'The couches and the furniture are mine. I'm pretty much handing over the rest of the house. She bought most of it and there's nothing much I want to keep.'

'Nothing?'

Finn shook his head. 'I'm not sentimental when it comes to stuff.'

He'd used to be but wasn't any more. Only with a gun

to his head would he admit that he'd kept all the sonar scan pictures of his baby—the baby that hadn't made it past four and a half months. Finn swallowed and steeled himself against the wave of pain. Okay, maybe he was a little sentimental about some things.

He pulled in a deep, restorative breath and along with it Callie's sweet perfume. She smelled so sweet and fresh, and he realised that *he* had to smell as if he'd been working his tail off all day—which he had—so he backed away from her.

'There's some wine or beer in the fridge—glasses in the cupboard next to the fridge. Help yourself. I'm just going to take a quick shower, if that's okay.'

'Sure, take your time.' Callie grinned at him. 'It'll give me time to snoop.'

'Snoop away—you won't find anything interesting,' Finn told her, before belting up the stairs to the en-suite bathroom off the guest bedroom.

As per normal, he glanced at the closed door of the room on the left and sighed. He really should try to move back into the master bedroom again. But he still hadn't replaced the mattress on their—*his*—bed, so what was the point? Maybe after he came back from his 'honeymoon' he'd try again.

Maybe. Or maybe he'd just get a whole new bed.

She liked Finn's house, Callie decided, liked the openness and the space. And the view was one of the best she'd seen. But the lack of anything personal surprised her; Finn was a world traveller—surely he would have picked up a memento here and there? Art? Pottery? Photographs?

Nothing in the house suggested that he'd lived here on an ongoing and permanent basis with his fiancée. Which was weird—weren't houses supposed to be shared? Granted, she wasn't an expert on co-habiting, but shouldn't the house be a place of compromise? Shouldn't there be a photograph of his family…his brothers? A trophy? A flat screen TV? Books…? Something that suggested that this was his house as much as hers?

For Finn's sake she hoped that his ex hadn't been an 'everything that's mine is mine and what's yours is mine too' type of woman. Maybe his priorities were a big screen TV and an internet connection—she'd dated more than a few men like that. Or maybe he simply wasn't a sentimental, collect-mementos-along-the-way type of guy.

Callie turned when she heard his footsteps behind her and saw that Finn had showered and dressed in a pair of black athletic shorts and a plain red T-shirt.

He ran his hands over his wet curls and sent her a small smile. 'Did you get some wine?'

'I didn't get that far.' Callie followed him into the kitchen and stood on the other side of a granite counter as he opened a cupboard door to pull out a glass. 'You look very fit—do you go to the gym?

Finn pulled a face. 'No. Martial arts.' He opened the fridge and she saw that it held nothing but a bottle of unopened wine, a mouldy block of cheese and some eggs. Someone hadn't been cooking or had been living on takeout.

Not healthy.

'What type of martial arts?' she asked, resisting the urge to mention his lack of food. Even if she was going to be his 'wife', she wasn't in a position to nag him about eating properly and taking care of himself. But, damn, she wanted to.

'Pretty much everything, actually. But I concentrate on Taekwondo and jiu-jitsu, occasionally taking a side trip into Krav Maga—'

'Notoriously difficult—out of the Israeli army.' She saw

the surprise flicker in his eyes at her even knowing about Krav Maga—but, hey, she read. A lot. 'Are you ranked?'

'You are the nosiest woman I've ever met,' Finn complained—not for the first and, she knew, not for the last time.

'And—I'll say it again—you're one of the few men who don't like talking about themselves.'

'So why do you keep asking?'

''Cos you're *fascinating*,' Callie replied, shoving her tongue into her cheek.

'Flirt.'

Callie dropped into a quick curtsy. 'Thank you, sir. So, what's your rank?'

Same question, phrased another way. His quick smile and the elaborate roll of his eyes told her that he was enjoying their banter. It would do him good to laugh, to smile.

'I'm ranked highly.'

She sighed dramatically at his answer. 'Trying to get information out of you is like trying to get blood out of a stone.' Callie took her glass of wine and sipped. 'Why don't you buy mementos of the places you've been?'

He blinked at the change of subject as he twisted the top off a bottle of beer. 'What? Like tourist tat?'

Callie sent him a patient look. 'Come on, Finn. Like you, I travel a lot and I know what is tat and what is art. And *everybody* sees something along the way that calls to them. I picked up a stunning vase in Murano that I treasure, a piece of street art in Rome. What do *you* buy?' She gestured to the soulless house. 'This is your house—why isn't there anything of you in it?'

Finn took a long sip of beer. 'You're going to nag me until I tell you, aren't you?'

'Actually, if it's a touchy or personal subject I won't. I know that I'm relentless, and curious, but I do respect your right not to talk. Just say *pass* and we'll move on.'

Callie shook her head and caught his look of surprise. 'This agreement we have doesn't include sharing our secrets. Well, you're welcome to share yours but I'm not sharing mine.'

Finn raised the bottle to his lips again and shook his head looking bewildered. That was okay, Callie thought. Bewildered she could live with. Annoyed or bored would make her think that she'd overstepped the mark.

'So why is there nothing personal in your house?' Callie grinned at his exasperation. 'What? You didn't say pass!'

'You are going to drive me crazy—I can just tell.' Finn closed his eyes and scratched the spot between his eyebrows. 'When I bought the house Liz moved in. She travelled as well, but she spent six weeks away and then a month at home. Her schedule was set but I could be away for two months, home for a week and gone again. She asked me time and time again to help her decorate the house—but, hell, I'm a guy. I'd rather watch sport or...watch paint dry. So one day she dumped all my stuff and all her stuff in the middle of the lounge—right over there—in front of the TV. There was a rugby match I wanted to watch so we had to sort through it. The whole process made me realise...'

'Pray tell?' Callie's lips quirked when he paused for dramatic effect.

'...that I buy crap and shouldn't be allowed anywhere near art galleries or home décor shops. If it's cheap and nasty, tasteless and fake, I *will* buy it.'

Callie's laughed bounced off the walls, and she was still chuckling when Finn led the way to the veranda, where Callie took a seat on an antique bench that had been converted into a swing.

'It's really better for everyone if I just hand over my credit card. Nobody gets hurt that way.'

Finn took a seat on a cane chair and propped his feet

up on the coffee table. After a minute of comfortable silence he spoke again.

'So, you said that there were things we needed to discuss?'

'I did.' Callie kicked off her sandals and felt comfortable enough to tuck her feet under her bottom on the denim
fabric of the swing. 'I put in for a month's holiday today,
and I also managed to organise it so that I don't have to
fly to Paris this week. So I am, in the most virginal sense,
all yours until we go.'

'That makes it easier, because there are a couple of
things we need to sort out before we go.'

'Like?'

'Like the lawyers for the magazine would like you to
sign an indemnity form, and they'd also like you to go for
a full medical—just to cover their legal asses.'

Callie wrinkled her nose. 'What a pain.'

'I use the same travel clinic all the time. I'll make an
appointment for you.' Finn rested his beer bottle on his
flat stomach. 'You'll need clothes that are suitable for five
and six-star resorts—'

Callie looked down at her designer sundress and lifted
her eyebrows. 'Finn, I am a fashion buyer—I think I have
the clothes covered.'

'Glad *you* do,' Finn grumbled, looking frustrated and
miserable. 'Because I sure don't. I keep thinking that I
have to get my act together and I keep putting it off. I hate
clothes-shopping.'

'You always looked okay to me.' Better than okay—
mighty fine, in fact. And his clothes were nice, too. 'So,
does your ineptitude with home decoration extend to your
wardrobe?'

Finn tipped his bottle up to lips. 'Yep. In spring and autumn Liz would drag my ass to the shops. She'd choose
and I'd pay.'

Callie's lips quirked. Shopping was something she *could* help him with. After taking a big sip of wine, she stood up and jerked her head, indicating that he should get up too. 'Let's go.'

'Where?'

'Up to your bedroom.'

When she saw his eyes widen and a gleam appear, she rolled her eyes and thought that she should explain—quickly.

'Since you're giving me an all-expenses-paid holiday, the least I can do is to help you out with your wardrobe. I'll go through your clothes, pick out what's suitable, and then we'll go shopping for what you need.'

Finn looked suddenly and momentarily panicked, but she put it down to the fact that no man—especially one as masculine as Finn—wanted to spend any part of his evening discussing clothes.

'Trust me…it'll be painless.'

'I don't think that having you in my bedroom is a very good idea,' Finn stated as he followed her through the house and up the stairs.

'We're taking it slow, one day at a time, and today is not *that* day, Banning,' Callie told him as they hit the top floor. 'Where's your bedroom?''

Finn gestured wordlessly to the closed door on their right. Callie opened it and walked into a white-on-cream, endlessly pale bedroom. Placing her hands on her hips, she lifted her eyebrows as she took in the cream and white striped walls, the deep beige curtains and the neutrally shaded pillows piled high on the floor.

She felt as if she'd stepped into a dairy.

'Wow…' she murmured.

'I hate this room,' Finn muttered, standing at the door, glaring.

'It's not that bad…it just needs some colour,' Callie

said, forcing herself to sound cheerful. She gestured to the bed—a white wood canopied monstrosity that dominated the room. 'You must also have hated the mattress.'

'What?' Finn barked.

'The mattress—it's gone.'

Finn shoved both hands into his hair and dropped his head, for a brief instant looking like a little boy who'd been slapped. Then his face changed and turned hard and determined.

'You know what? Let's not worry about checking what I have that I can take. I'll just buy a whole new wardrobe.'

Callie started to argue, but stopped when she saw the misery underneath the fury. 'That's an expensive exercise,' she said carefully, knowing that there was something fundamental that she was missing.

'I can afford it,' Finn said and gestured for her to leave the room.

Callie knew that it wasn't the right time to argue with him, to try and push his buttons. He wanted her out for some deeply private reason, so she left the bedroom and headed for the stairs. She waited until they were halfway down before speaking again.

'Still want me to help you shop for clothes?'

Finn's tension seemed to fade as he closed the door behind him. His white teeth flashed. 'Hell, yes. I might come back with one of those khaki vests with a hundred pockets and pants that unzip at the knees to become shorts.'

Callie shuddered at the thought, not entirely convinced he was joking. 'You *definitely* need help.'

Finn's broad hand, warm and exciting, encircled her neck as they walked down the stairs. 'In more ways than one. So, what are we ordering for supper?'

She loved spending other people's money, Callie thought, holding up two shirts for Finn that she really liked. And it was so much fun shopping for a guy. Finn didn't think so, but she did. They'd only been at it for a couple of hours and he was starting to wilt—the lightweight.

There was a pile of bags in Finn's SUV already, and with the clothes now on a low couch in this store she thought he would have everything he might need for the next couple of weeks—possibly years. She'd made him buy belts and shorts, designer tees and shirts, shoes and ties, and she'd had a blast.

'Anything else, Callie?'

You knew you were a professional shopper when the sales clerks knew you by name, Callie thought. 'No, I think that's it, Annie. If you'd like to start ringing that pile up, I'll take these to Finn so that he can try them on. We'll meet you at the counter in a few.'

'Sounds like a plan,' Annie agreed, and Callie left her to gather up the clothes while she walked into the three-cubicle dressing room, the shirts over her arm.

The first two were empty, and she skidded to a halt as she saw Finn's reflection in the third changing room mirror through a gap in the curtains.

She couldn't pull her gaze away from the perfection that was his body. He was wearing nothing more than a brief pair of pants, and his body rippled with muscle as he shoved a shirt back onto a hanger. His legs were long and muscled, his tanned shoulders broad, his butt round and tight. His broad chest and rippled stomach made all the saliva in her mouth disappear.

How was she supposed to go on holiday with him, knowing how much she wanted him? This gnawing need to know what he felt like, how he made love, how he would feel as he filled her, completed her, was unusual for her, and it scared her as nothing else ever had. Yes, she needed to explore his body—but she also wanted to dig below his cool, calm and controlled surface to see what was underneath.

That wasn't good. She always kept her distance from men who made her feel too much, who intrigued her. They were dangerous. They made her want more than sex, more than a brief affair, and nobody had made her want more like Finn did.

It didn't matter how much she wanted him, she reminded herself. She could want and wish and pray, but the people she needed to stick around never did. *Remember?*

That cold dose of reality didn't make her desire for Finn disappear. Her mind might realise that he was dangerous but her body still craved him.

She could never allow herself to risk getting to know him too well. She couldn't get emotionally attached to him. But she wanted to know his touch, his taste, how it felt to have that powerful body giving and receiving pleasure.

Finn's eyes met hers in the mirror and he just stared at her, half naked, his desire for her blazing from his face. She watched, fascinated, as his penis grew into an erection from nothing more than looking at her. Finn didn't try to hide his reaction. Instead he just kept his eyes locked on hers, his hands on his hips.

'Keeping my hands off you is going to be a problem,' he said, his voice low and slow. He turned to face her and yanked the curtains open.

Callie licked her lips and shook her head, trying to be sensible.

'I'm not thinking of my failed engagement or my ex. I promise that I am not thinking of anyone but you,' Finn growled.

She heard the frustration and the truth in his voice. He wanted her—possibly as much as she did him.

How was he able to look inside her head and see what she was thinking? He seemed to be able to intuit immediately and correctly what she was thinking without her saying a word.

Nobody had ever managed to do that before.

'Too soon,' Callie stated, sighing as she felt her panties dampen. 'It really is, Finn.'

An F-bomb shattered the loaded silence between them and then Finn's hand shot out and grabbed her wrist. Yanking her into the cubicle, he jerked the curtains shut and the shirts she held fell to the floor.

Finn took her chin in his hand and tipped her head up. 'Have you ever stood in front of a fire and wanted to be in the heart of it? Inside the colours…the heat? Yeah, you have—because that's how you were looking at me just now. Like I was the fire and you wanted to feel my heat. You want me…'

She wanted to deny it but she couldn't. Of course she wanted him—she'd been fantasising about him for months. But it was just lust and attraction and the fact that she hadn't had an orgasm in far too long.

Didn't she deserve to feast on him just a little?

'It's just lust. I haven't felt it for a while,' she told him.

'It's a crazy chemical reaction. But we can handle a little chemistry, can't we?'

Yes—no. Maybe… What did she know? Her brain had long since shut down.

'So let's test the theory. Kiss me, lose yourself in my mouth. Right here, right now. Let me taste all of your heat, your passion.'

How could she say no? A hot, no-holds-barred kiss? She wanted it as much as he did. Just to test the theory, of course. People had sex-based relationships all the time— hell, *she'd* had sex-based relationships all her adult life. What was so different about Finn? *Nothing,* she resolutely lied to herself. Yes, he was hot—yes, he set her nerve-endings on fire—yes, he made her lady bits squirm. But she'd had good-looking men before. She'd handled them and she'd handle Finn Banning.

She would—even if it killed her. And this was her chance to prove it.

Then Finn's mouth covered hers and she realised that she was right to be hesitant, right to be a little scared. Because she'd never been held like this, touched liked this—*God*, tasted like this.

His arms were strong, his hands tender, one on her hip, the other holding the back of her head, keeping her mouth to his. She could feel the heat of his bare chest as her breasts smashed against it, could feel his erection brushing her stomach, hard and wonderful. But his mouth...

She would never get enough of his taste, of the way he sipped and then suckled and then, to mix it up, swirled his tongue around hers. He gently bit her bottom lip, then soothed the sting away with a swipe of his tongue. And while his mouth was busy decimating hers his hand started to explore her body.

She felt his fingers moving over the bumps of her spine, drifting across her bottom, sneaking under her skirt to feel the backs of her thighs, tracing her thong where it disappeared between her butt cheeks. He skimmed her happy place, and when she wiggled against his hand slid his finger under the cotton to her entrance, slipping through the heat and wet to that tiny bundle of nerves.

Callie felt her knees buckle and Finn instantly tightened his arm around her back, plastering her to him as her legs widened, allowing him deeper access. One finger, then two, and his thumb was brushing her clitoris.

'You feel so amazing...' Finn muttered against her mouth, green eyes blazing.

'We should stop.'

'Hell, no,' Finn muttered. 'Just this once...don't think... just lose yourself.'

'We can't have sex in a changing room cubicle, Finn,' Callie protested, trying to being sensible.

'We're not going to make love. You're just going to come, and I'm going to watch you fall apart in my arms.'

'I can't—'

'Yeah, you can—and you will,' Finn told her, hooking a small stool with his foot and dragging it over to them.

Turning Callie around, he placed her hands on the mirror before lifting her right foot up onto the stool. Bunching her skirt in one hand, he lifted it slowly to reveal her lacy thong. He pulled it to one side and stared at her waxed strip, tracing it with one finger before sliding that finger into her folds. Callie watched, turned on, as he started to pleasure her, sliding his finger over her clitoris and into her vagina in a slow, steady, orgasm-building rhythm.

His other hand came up to undo the buttons of her shirt, leaving it to fall open and show a hint of her ivory bra. His tanned hand was dark against her lighter skin—and then it disappeared beneath the cup of her bra to cover her breast. Instantly her nipple swelled into his palm, demanding attention.

His fingers worked in tandem to devastate her control—fingers in her panties and fingers rubbing her nipple—and soon she couldn't help her harsh breathing as she climbed up and up, reaching for that ultimate release, that burst of concentrated pleasure that she hadn't experienced in far too long…

'Look at you…so hot, so close,' Finn growled in her ear. 'See how beautiful you are.'

Callie almost didn't recognise the woman in the mirror—the one standing in Finn's arms. Her hair was messy, her face flushed, and her eyes were a deep, dark mesmerising blue. She looked wild and out of control.

'You're so frickin' hot I could come just looking at you.'

Finn pushed another finger into her channel and flicked her clit with his thumb. Callie shuddered in his arms.

'Come for me. Right now.'

At his command Callie fell apart in his arms, instinctively bucking against his fingers as she milked every last sensation from the experience. From a place far away, where fireworks were exploding inside her brain, she felt Finn stiffen against her, his erection against her back. She heard his low moan and then felt the hand that was on her breast leave her to grab himself, covering his penis as he turned away and came into the palm of his hand.

In a shop's dressing room. In the middle of the day. *Dear God.*

His muttered curse bounced off the walls of the dressing room and pulled her back from that happy place.

'I haven't done that since I was a horny teenager.' He sent her a hot, frustrated, embarrassed look. 'Apparently I have absolutely no control around you.'

Ditto, Callie thought. She rested her head against the mirror as he backed away from her, aftershocks still skittering through her body. The fact that they—two people who'd been around the block, the world—had no 'off' button when they touched was a huge warning that they should keep their distance.

She couldn't handle him—this. This nuclear reaction couldn't be controlled so it should be contained, and the only way to contain it was not to light the fuse.

She needed control. Control made her feel safe and secure. Control meant that her mind and emotions could stand apart and let her body have its fun. If all three got in on the action, as they had minutes before, then she was toast.

Finn quickly shucked his underwear, giving her a quick peek at a black thatch of hair and his still mostly erect penis. He swore as he used his underwear to clean up. 'That was *not* supposed to happen.'

'I don't think any of it was,' Callie said, closing her eyes.

She heard him stepping into his jeans, the rasp of the zip, a long sigh.

'Are you okay?'

Callie opened her eyes and stepped away from the mirror. She smoothed down her skirt as Finn pulled on his T-shirt.

Finn sent her a long, concerned look as he repeated his question. 'Callie, talk to me. Are you okay?'

Callie looked up at the ceiling. 'Yeah. Wow. Yes. But I think that we should get going. They're going to come looking for us soon.'

On cue, Annie's hesitant voice drifted from the entrance of the fitting rooms. 'Callie? Everything all right?'

Callie's lips twitched as she replied. 'We're coming!'

Finn started to grin. and Callie slapped his shoulder in warning. 'If you say *Been there, done that* I swear I will slap you!'

CHAPTER FIVE

FINN STEERED HIS SUV into the empty parking space in front of Callie's front door and frowned when he saw the tall blond guy sitting on her front step.

'I thought you said you were single,' he said to her bent head. He didn't like the fact that white-hot jealousy speared through him. The thought of any other man having her, being with her, while the delicious scent of her was still on his fingers, the memory of her falling apart in his arms was still so fresh, made him feel ill.

Callie picked up her head and frowned. 'I am. Why?'

He glared at the man—who just looked at them, waiting for them to leave the car. 'Pissed off male sitting on your steps.'

Callie looked out through the front windshield and pursed her lips. 'Older brother.'

Ah. Relief—which was bizarre, because he had no claim to this woman. 'Can he wait five minutes? We need to talk.'

Callie sat back and nodded. Finn ignored her brother's thundercloud face and turned in his seat to face her, making sure that the windows were up so no part of this conversation could leak from the car.

He thought about how to start, what exactly he wanted to say. They hadn't spoken since leaving the shopping mall and he thought that they needed to clear the air before this went any further.

'So, a little chemistry, huh?'

Callie broke the tense silence, verbalising his thoughts. How did she manage to do that?

'If you can call that explosion "a little chemistry",' Finn muttered, wanting to bang his forehead against the steering wheel. 'That was crazy. I've never...' Finn swallowed his embarrassment. 'Never lost it like that before. We had hot sex in a changing room, Callie!'

'Well, it wasn't really...' Callie blew air into her cheeks. 'Yeah.'

Callie's tongue touched the centre of her top lip and he held back his groan and cursed the stirring in his pants.

'This was supposed to be a simple arrangement!' he muttered, more to himself than to her.

'It's still simple,' Callie argued. 'We're going on holiday together, I'm going to pretend to be your wife, and we're going to end up in bed sooner or later. And, judging by that craziness, probably sooner.'

'I'm old enough to know that explosive sex has a way of making stuff extraordinarily complicated.'

'We're also old enough to work our way around that,' she said.

Finn frowned at her as he stared at her profile. '*Whoah*... Let me get this straight. Are you saying that you are *happy* to have sex? You said you wanted to take it day by day.'

Callie blushed and threw her hands up in the air. 'I don't know what to think! I'm still in orgasm land! And I'm still wrapping my head around the fact that we did *that*, in a semi-public place, at noon, in a busy shop where I know the sales ladies.'

She buried her face in her hands.

'I'm never going to be able to go back in there. They *knew*, Finn!' Callie pushed her fingers into her hair as she lifted her head. 'We didn't give where we were and what we were doing a moment's thought, Finn. Hell, we didn't think *at all*!'

We didn't think at all... Her words made him push back into the seat, his breath hitching. That was it—exactly it. The biggest problem he had around this woman was that he didn't think. He just had to put his hands on that warm skin, had to kiss that luscious mouth, and his freaking brain switched off.

And he needed to think—needed time not only to work through the runaway fire that was currently his life but also why she had the ability to short circuit his thought processes. He needed to think about how he was going to handle this craziness between them so that neither of them ended up scalded.

Callie stared out of the window. 'Would you prefer that I didn't come with you?

'No! Where the hell did *that* come from?' Finn shot back, panicked at the thought of her backing out. And not only because he needed a 'wife' so he could do his job.

Finn let out a long stream of air. Dammit, it was his turn to be sensible, to take a step back from the situation and use his brain. His big brain.

He needed some distance from her; his body needed to get closer but *he* needed space to think.

'Maybe we should just get through the next couple of days, get on the road and, as you said, see what happens—okay?'

Since Callie looked relieved at this reprieve, he knew that it was the right decision, that he was on the right track.

'Okay.'

Callie nodded, but her next words surprised the hell out of him. Whatever else he'd expected her to say it wasn't this:

'And still no hearts and flowers at the end?'

Finn nodded his agreement. 'Definitely not.' He gestured to her brother, whose look had now passed pissed off and was on its way to furious. 'You'd better go—he's been waiting long enough.'

Callie wrinkled her nose. 'Yeah.' She opened the door and swung her legs out of the car. 'Hey, Seb.'

'Callie. Is that who you're running away with? Want to introduce us?'

Finn heard the whipped out words before Callie slammed the door behind her. Hitting the button to take down his electric window, he made a production of putting his seat belt on before starting the car.

'No, I am *not* going to introduce you. Why are you here?'

'We need to talk about Laura and why you're running off with some stranger to avoid seeing her,' the brother stated as Callie brushed past him to her front door.

Finn, not able to delay his departure any longer without being caught out, reversed and sent a last look at her.

Who was Laura and why was Callie running from her? And why was he so curious to find out all he could about her? And why did he hate the stricken look he'd seen on her face when her brother had mentioned Laura's name?

It was the journalist in him, he told himself as he accelerated away. It was his job to be curious—about people as well as places.

And apparently, he thought as he turned the corner, his job now also included deception and lying to himself as well.

Crazy.

In her lounge, Callie tossed her bag onto the couch and faced her brother, hands on her hips. 'I don't appreciate you rocking up on my doorstep unannounced and looking for a fight.'

Seb, tall and strong and looking as frustrated as she

felt, pushed his fists into the pockets of his jeans. 'When my sister storms out of her house—'

'*Your* house.'

Seb glared at her interruption. '*Her* house and refuses to take my calls for three days I am allowed to rock up here and have it out with you. We're all worried about you.'

'So I hear,' Callie retorted. 'Apparently my life is now too good and I am too independent. I remember a time when you thought the exact opposite. There's just no pleasing you, is there, big bro?'

'That happened a long time ago and it has no bearing on this situation. Look, Ro and I—'

Ro and I. It had used to be *Callie and Ro.* They'd used to be a team—best friends. Had Seb driven a wedge between her and her best friend? Had he surpassed her in importance? It was natural if he had, but Rowan had always been her rock, her sounding board, her port in a storm. Now she was Seb's.

Callie had never felt so alone in her life. Oh, wait, maybe she had. For the first couple of months after Laura had left. First couple of months, years, most of her life...

You're being silly and sentimental and emotional, Callie thought as she walked over to the doors to the veranda and yanked them open, looking for some air. It had been a crazy couple of days—culminating with a very hot, very sexy, very confusing encounter in that dressing room— and she was exhausted and played out. Ro was still Ro, and she still loved her, but it just didn't feel as if anyone was standing in *her* corner right now.

But that was okay. It was time to pull on her big girl panties and kick some ass. And her brother was a great target.

Callie leaned against the frame of the now open door and turned back to him. 'Look, Seb, I absolutely understand and respect your right to talk to your mother, and I'd appreciate it if you'd respect my right not to.'

'She's your mother too. Don't you at least want to know why she left?' Seb demanded.

So like Seb, Callie thought. Analytical and clear-thinking. If he understood the cause he could make sense of the problem. For her it was a lot more simple —cut and dried.

'She left you and me—bottom line. I don't care what her reason was. She left. When you have kids you put *them* first, not yourself.'

'In one of her letters she said that her life was overwhelming—that was why she retreated to her room, why she eventually left.'

Callie threw her hands up in the air in exasperation at his explanation. 'Overwhelming? God, Seb, she was a stay-at-home mother with a housekeeper and a rich husband who spoilt her rotten. That's a stupid excuse. There are millions of women all over the world who have a lot less, who live in terrible circumstances, and who don't walk out on their kids.'

Seb shrugged. 'I don't disagree with you, but I still think that I need to meet with her—that *you* need to meet with her. To hear her side and to find closure, if nothing else.'

'I don't need closure. I'm perfectly fine,' Callie said stubbornly.

'All your issues are rooted in Laura leaving,' Seb stated, still pushing.

Callie ground her teeth together, trying to keep a hold on her bubbling temper. 'I do *not* have issues!'

Seb snorted. 'Honey, you delude yourself. You're crazy independent because you refuse to rely on anyone in case they let you down. You're consistently single because you don't trust anyone to be there long-term.'

From the couch Callie heard the strident ring tone of

her mobile and she walked over to answer the call, grateful for the interruption and the opportunity to get hold of her temper before she slapped her brother.

She saw Rowan's name on the display and barked a tense greeting.

'My fiancé there?' Rowan asked, after saying hello.

Callie answered in the affirmative and Rowan ordered her to put her on speaker phone. Callie shrugged, did what she said and held up the mobile in her hand.

'Seb!' Rowan's voice sounded frustrated. 'What did I say to you?'

Seb grimaced. 'I know, but—'

'Leave your sister alone. If she doesn't want to meet Laura, then it's her decision—not yours.'

'But—'

Rowan didn't give him a chance to explain. 'We spoke about this. We agreed that you would leave her alone! *God!*'

'But—'

'Respect her right to make her own decisions, Hollis.'

After that bombshell Rowan told Callie to take her off speaker phone, and Callie lifted her phone to her ear, watching as her brother threw his hands up in the air.

'As per usual, you two have ganged up on me. I'm out of here,' Seb stated, before turning and heading for the front door.

'He's left and he's not happy,' Callie told Rowan, not feeling quite so alone as before.

Callie could imagine Rowan's shrug. 'So? I might love him to distraction, but he's still messing with my best friend and nobody—not even him—does that. I'm the only one with that privilege.'

Callie felt tears prick her eyes. 'I love you, you know.'

'I love you too, kiddo.' Rowan sighed. 'I just need to ask you one question.'

'Okay.'

'Do you know what you're doing, Cal?'

Callie sank into the corner of the couch and tipped her head back. 'I don't have the foggiest idea. Can you come over? I need you.'

'On my way.'

Maybe, Callie thought as she placed her mobile on the couch next to her, she wasn't quite as alone as she'd thought.

Callie, her bags in a pile next to the door, pulled open the front door and sucked in her breath as she caught sight of her fake husband. Finn was dressed for travelling in a pair of lightweight grey linen shorts and a black and white checked shirt over a snow-white T-shirt that skimmed his broad chest. His arms were muscled and tanned, and the only jewellery he wore was a high-tech watch that could probably launch spaceships.

His eyes widened when he saw her. 'You look fantastic, fake wife.'

Callie grinned at him. 'Thank you.'

Callie knew that she looked good in the pink-orchid-coloured swing dress with its copper leather belt and drawstring neck. She'd kept her accessories and make-up minimal, and she wore flat, gold sequinned sandals. She knew she looked the part of a stylish woman about to embark on her honeymoon.

Did she have everything for her bogus honeymoon? Clothes—check. Passport—check. Accessories and toiletries—check. Jewellery, simple, classy, to go with all her outfits—check.

Except for one glaringly obvious exception... Hell, she wasn't wearing a wedding ring!

Finn caught her expression and frowned. 'What's wrong?'

'Your fake wife needs a fake ring,' she said, lifting her arm and wiggling the fingers of her left hand.

Finn twisted his lips as he stepped into her hallway and wound his way around her bags. 'I didn't even think of that.' He looked at his watch and sighed his annoyance. 'Liz still has the engagement ring I bought her.'

Callie's mouth dropped open. 'I am *not* wearing your ex's ring!'

A shallow dimple appeared in Finn's cheek. 'You're pretty picky for a wife who isn't actually my wife!'

Callie lifted her nose. 'I still have standards—fake or not.'

Finn sighed. 'I suppose we could pick up something at the airport.'

Callie lifted her eyebrows. The only jewellery stores at the airport were high-end and very expensive, and she couldn't justify him splurging for a ring that she'd only wear for three weeks. She quickly did a mental stroll through her jewellery collection in the hope that she had something remotely engagement-ring-like. Then she remembered the large velvet jewellery box Seb had left with her just after he'd got engaged to Rowan.

'It's mostly Grandma's jewellery, with a couple of pieces our mother left behind,' he'd said. 'You should have them.'

Callie hadn't wanted to keep the box and she'd never bothered to look inside. It was still at the back of her lingerie drawer, where she'd shoved it a year or so ago.

She still didn't want to open it, but this was an emergency.

'How much time have we got before we have to leave?' she asked Finn as she turned towards the stairs.

'A half hour or so,' Finn replied. 'Why? Do you have some diamond rings stashed upstairs?'

'Maybe,' Callie replied, hearing Finn's footsteps behind

her. She turned, faced him, and for once they were eye to eye. 'It might be better if you stay down here.'

'Why?'

'My room. It's a bit messy.' *Catastrophic* was a better word, Callie thought.

'I've seen messy before,' Finn told her.

'Not like this, you haven't,' Callie assured him. Seeing the stubborn look on his face, she sighed and shrugged. 'Don't say I didn't warn you.'

Dear God! Finn looked around the master bedroom, his mouth open wide enough to catch flies. Who had so many clothes and why were they scattered everywhere?

When he managed to find his voice, he croaked the words out. 'Newsflash, Callie: clothes can be put back into cupboards as well as taken out.'

Callie stepped over a pile of shoes as she headed to her dresser. 'No point,' she said over her shoulder. 'While I was trying to decide what to pack I realised that I have far too many clothes—'

'Seriously? I would never have guessed that!' Finn said from the doorway, thinking that if he went in he might not find his way out. *Ever.*

Callie ignored his interruption. 'And I decided that I need to clean out my wardrobe. That pile is for Rowan, that pile is for the secondhand shop, and that pile is to be donated.' She waved her hands around the room.

Finn leaned a shoulder into the doorframe and crossed his arms. 'Damn...' he muttered again.

Callie yanked open a drawer in her dresser and Finn's mouth went dry as she tossed a pile of rainbow-coloured thongs and bras onto a chair. They were skimpy and frothy and ultra-feminine.

'I get samples from the designers I do business with,' Callie said, seemingly oblivious to the fact that he was mentally stripping her in an attempt to see what she wearing under that sexy, stylish dress.

It would probably be the same sexy deep pink, he decided. Callie was nothing if not colour co-ordinated.

'I can't remember when last I actually went to a store and bought clothes. That's why I had so much fun shopping for you.'

With difficulty Finn raised his eyes to her face and tried to look as if he had heard her. But he was a guy—distract him with sexy lingerie and his brain headed south. With his blood. And his hearing.

'Ah—got it.'

Finn watched as Callie pulled out a large jewellery box and, cradling it in both hands, walked back towards him. She skirted the bed and sat on the side closest to him, on top of a pile of jackets, putting the box down next to her. A wistful, sad, wary look passed across her face and he straightened, all thoughts of sex and lingerie gone. This box meant something to her, and he wasn't sure if it was a good or bad something. Probably a mixture of both.

Then, very surprisingly, she stood up, picked up the box and thrust it towards him. Finn caught it as it hit his chest and she dropped it from her grasp.

'Look in there and see if you can find something that I can wear. If there isn't anything then I'm afraid you're out of luck. I'll be downstairs.'

Finn frowned as she slipped past him and ran down the stairs. Putting the box on the bedside table, he switched on the light and flipped the lid. His breath caught at the blink of gold inside. It was a pirate's treasure box, he thought, bubbling with thick gold chains and bracelets and the occasional flash of a precious stone in a pendant.

Lifting up a handful of chains, silver and gold, some with pendants and some without, he saw that there were smaller boxes below and dumped the chains on the bed.

The first box held earrings—mostly old-fashioned, but there was a nice pair of diamond studs he could see Callie wearing. The next box held rings, and he pulled in his breath as he ran his fingers over the jewels.

Of the eight or so in the box there were at least four that would pass as engagement rings, and three had matching wedding bands. One ring fascinated him: it looked older than the others—a big diamond, with spikes of platinum radiating in another circle embedded with tiny diamonds. A thin band sat under the diamond and he presumed that was a wedding band.

Finn held it under the light and on the inside could just make out the date: June the sixth, 1909.

That'll do, he thought, tucking it into the pocket of his pants.

He quickly replaced the boxes he'd taken out and dumped the tangle of chains back inside the larger box. Snapping the lid shut, he walked across to the near empty cupboard, found a shoebox and tossed the shoes inside on to the floor. Sliding the jewellery box into the shoebox, he used his height to stretch up and hide the box behind another pile of shoeboxes.

He wondered why he was bothering. If any thieves broke in and found themselves in Callie's bedroom while she was away they'd think she'd been ransacked already and leave.

Finn tried to close the cupboard doors and wondered why Callie wouldn't deal with the box herself. Why would a woman who obviously loved clothes—and, he presumed, accessories—ignore a box full of such amazing jewellery? Why couldn't she even open it to look inside for a ring she needed?

Strange. But interesting. Curiosity, he reminded himself, and he didn't need to indulge it. Not where Callie was concerned.

Finn rubbed the back of his neck, thinking that she couldn't do the jewellery box and he couldn't do his bedroom. Maybe they deserved each other.

Finn left the room and jogged down the stairs. He found Callie sitting on a chair in her hallway, legs crossed and her foot jiggling.

She looked up at him with those amazing reticent eyes. 'Did you find something?'

'Lots of things,' Finn said, keeping his voice easy. 'That's quite a little treasure trove you've got there. That box should be in a safe, by the way.'

Callie lifted a bare shoulder. 'I wouldn't know. I've never looked inside.'

'Why not?' Finn asked the question although he knew that she wouldn't answer.

'It's complicated and I have my reasons.' Callie stood up and held out her hand. 'Let's see it.'

Finn pulled the two rings from his pocket and dropped them into her hand. He watched as she stared at them. She looked as though she was trying to place them, but after she'd given the tiniest shake to her head she picked the wedding ring up to take a closer look.

'It's really pretty.'

'It has a date in 1909 inscribed on the band,' Finn told her.

'It must be my great-grandmother's—Seb told me that some of the family pieces were in the box,' Callie replied, sliding both rings over the ring finger on her left hand. 'They fit. Yay.'

'Good.' Finn smiled lazily. 'That was easily sorted. Just promise me you'll get the box into a safe deposit box or just a safe. There were quite a few bigger and better diamonds and precious stones than that one.'

Callie shifted on her feet. 'Maybe.' She nudged a suitcase with her foot. 'Shall we go?'

'Yep.' Finn looked at the pile of suitcases on the floor and sighed. Okay, they were going for a while, but two large cases and a carry-on seemed a bit excessive. But judging by what had been left behind she probably thought that this was—what had she called it the other day?—a capsule wardrobe. He thought it looked like backache waiting for a place to happen.

'Okay, grab your stuff and I'll wait for you in the car,' he said, teasing her.

Callie looked surprised, then confused, and then her eyes cleared as he realised he was joking. 'Carry on like that and I'm going to cut you off from fake sex.'

Finn slung the tote bag over his shoulder and pulled the bigger of the two suitcases up onto its wheels. 'Fake married for two seconds,' he grumbled as she opened the front door for him, 'and I'm already on rations for sex I might not even get. This is a tough gig.'

'You were the one who wanted to get married,' Callie reminded him. 'Didn't I tell you that it was a bad idea? I'm sure I said something about it being a long stupidity...'

Six hours later Callie stood in the tasteful lobby of the Baobab and Buffalo, sipping a welcome glass of champagne while Finn took care of the details surrounding their stay at this first six-star resort.

According to their itinerary they would be staying in the honeymoon suite for one night before being moved to another room for the rest of their three-night stay. Since bookings at the Baobab and Buffalo were harder to come by than hen's teeth, and since this entire 'honeymoon' was sponsored—and fake—Callie knew that they were in no position to complain.

And, really, what was there to complain about? The resort was utterly fantastic. The main building was built in grey stone and lavishly but tastefully decorated. Judging by the discreet signs, there was a business room, a library, various lounges and dining rooms. Callie walked across the lobby, intrigued by the double-volume doors and the view beyond the glass.

Stepping onto the long veranda, she gasped at the endless view of bush beyond her. Wild and wondrous. There was a watering hole for wildlife at the bottom of the cliff below, and verdant green terraces led to an infinity pool that seemed to cling to the edge of the cliff.

Well, wow.

Callie turned at a touch on her shoulder. 'Mrs Banning?'

Callie turned and looked into the eyes of a gorgeous redhead. 'No. I'm Callie—' Then she remembered that she was supposed to be married and flushed with embarrassment. Her brain kicked up a gear as she tried to explain her gaffe. 'Sorry—I'm still operating on my own name.'

The redhead grinned. 'I absolutely understand; I'm recently married myself. I'm Clem—welcome to the Two B.'

Callie had read her fair share of celebrity magazines and instantly recognised this ex-model, who'd once been engaged to one of the world's most notorious musicians. From socialite to living on an upmarket game reserve. Now *that* was a life-change.

'Thank you. It's beautiful.'

Clem sighed. 'It really is. I'm still in awe of what Nick's managed to build here.'

Clem jammed her hands in her khaki shorts and gestured to a dark-haired man who stood at the other end of the veranda, talking to a man dressed in the same uniform of khaki shorts and navy polo shirt.

'That's Nick and his right-hand man, Jabu. They are the heart and soul of the Two B. Sorry, that's what we call this place. The Baobab and Buffalo is such a mouthful.'

Callie watched as Nick and his wife exchanged a look across the veranda that blazed with passion and lust. Callie felt as if she needed a fan or a long drink of water when they finally looked away from each other, but Clem turned back to Callie, acting as if she *hadn't* just eye-bonked her husband.

'What are you hoping to do here? Or are you just planning to hibernate in your room and...well, do what honeymooners do?'

How the hell was she supposed to answer that question? She didn't even know the answer to any of the questions *she* had with regard to her and Finn's relationship—the fake one or the real one!

Were they going to sleep with each other? *Duh.* That was a no-brainer—as soon as they had to share a bed they'd be all over each other...there was no way they'd be able to resist. And that would be the start of their three-week fling. It would be hot and sexy and rollercoaster-crazy and she had to remember to keep her emotional distance. *No spilling the secrets of your soul, Hollis!*

Callie frowned at the rogue thought. What was wrong with her? She had always been able to separate sex and emotion—why was she worried that she wouldn't be able to do it with Finn? *Because you like him,* Callie admitted reluctantly. *Because you'd like to be his friend, have him be yours.* And that meant taking a step away from being 'safe' and unattached; it would take her into uncharted territory...

'Callie?'

Callie blinked at her hostess. 'Sorry, I zoned out. Tired...'

Clem laughed and patted her arm again. 'No problem—I understand. I was so exhausted after my wedding day I could barely string a sentence together.'

Yeah, that wasn't it. Looking into Clem's beautiful, open, happy face, Callie felt the urge to spill her secrets.

Actually, I'm not really married. I'm running away from reconnecting with my long-absent mother.

And I want to sleep with Finn; he's exciting and intriguing and the first man in for ever who I can imagine myself falling for. But I'm scared that he's the one man that I will like more after I've slept with him—not less. I already like him more than I should. Hell, I knew that I liked him more than was wise on the plane home from JFK—and this is all very scary for me. And he's on the rebound and I never, repeat never, sleep with men I can fall for.

So I'm confused. And more than little terrified.

And I really don't like being either.

Callie suspected that Clem would understand.

Callie sighed her relief as she saw Finn walking towards them, a Two B butler two steps behind. She gathered her wits and made the introductions. 'Finn Banning—meet Clem. She and her husband own and run the Baobab and Buffalo.'

Clem's eyes narrowed slightly and her smile was a little cool. 'You're the journalist doing an article on us?'

Hmm, it seemed that the fiery redhead wasn't fond of journalists—then again, with her history with the profession Callie couldn't blame her.

'I am,' Finn said easily, his hand resting low on Callie's back, his fingers just above her butt cheek. It was a very possessive, familiar gesture—one perfectly suited to a newly married man.

'We don't normally allow reporters to write about the Two B; we're booked for years in advance and don't need the publicity. We're doing this as a favour to the owner of *Go Travel* who's a regular visitor.'

Clem kept the smile on her face but there was a note of protectiveness in her voice that was unmistakable. Finn's fingers flexed on Callie's back and Callie knew that he'd heard Clem's warning too.

Finn sent her an easy smile. 'I'm morally bound to write on my personal experiences and I already know that my experience here will be utterly fantastic. We're so lucky to start off our honeymoon here.'

Clem relaxed and Callie released her pent-up breath. Finn casually sipped from the glass of champagne he'd been handed on walking through the front door.

Clem nodded at the papers in his hand. 'I've tweaked your itinerary to showcase the best of what we can offer honeymooners—which is an utterly unique and memorable experience.' Clem pulled a face, humour back in her eyes. 'I'm sorry, it doesn't leave much time for long, lazy mornings spent in bed, but it will be exciting and amazing.'

Wow. If all the lodges were going to pull out the stops the way Clem was doing then Callie was in for one hell of a holiday.

'We're grateful for your personal touch,' said Mr Charmer at her side.

'Then Sarah, your personal butler, will take it from here. Enjoy your stay,' Clem said, before turning away to walk towards her husband.

Nick immediately opened his arms and Clem snuggled up into his side. Callie briefly wondered what it would feel like to love a man like that—to be loved like that. To feel so absolutely, utterly secure in yourself and in his love that you could slide into a conversation and into his arms without either of you missing a beat, as if it was the most natural action in the world.

Love, it seemed, could work for some. But Callie knew that she wasn't one of the lucky few. No, she was better off on her own, walking her own path.

That way she could be in control and could stop her heart from walking off the side of a cliff and splattering on the rocks below.

CHAPTER SIX

INSTEAD OF WALKING them to their room, as he'd expected, Sarah led Finn and Callie to an open game-viewing vehicle and invited them to climb inside. As he hoisted himself up into the vehicle he noticed that their luggage was neatly stowed in the back of the vehicle, just behind the second row of bench seats.

Finn settled himself next to Callie, conscious that the sun was starting to set and the temperature was falling; the day's heat was giving way to the chill of the first, unexpectedly early cold front, suggesting that autumn was just around the corner. Callie pulled out a shawl from her bag and wound it around her shoulders as Sarah accelerated away.

When they drove back through the impressive entrance Finn realised that they were leaving the security of the electric fenced estate and were heading into the reserve itself—wild and beautiful.

This is more like it, he thought, his eyes scanning the bush for signs of wildlife.

Within five hundred yards of the gate they saw a herd of springbok and a female warthog with her piglets. Then they saw a fish eagle in a tree, and Sarah pointed out a reclusive eland bull in a thicket of acacias.

This is Africa, he thought, breathing deeply. *The sounds and sights of the bush.*

A part of him wished that Sarah would dump them in a clearing and pull out a tent. He needed the solitude and peace of nature. After this crazy couple of weeks he wanted to wind down, and he couldn't think of a better way to do it than being alone in the bush. But because this was the Buffalo and Baobab he suspected that their idea of getting up close and personal with nature would be much better.

He'd barely finished that thought when Sarah veered off the dirt road onto a grassy track. Within a hundred metres she'd stopped in a clearing and Finn looked around.

They were on the edge of a cliff, and he could hear the muted sound of a river smacking on rocks below them. In one of the huge wild fig trees overlooking the river he could see a tree house, nestled into its strong branches. Except that it was less house and more platforms—three of them in all, staggered up the tree. The bottom platform looked to be a bathroom, complete with shower, the second held couches and a table, and the highest one, he presumed, would hold a bed. A bed that was open to the African sky and the elements.

Finn hopped out and slapped his hands on his hips, grinning wildly. 'Oh, this is so cool! But what happens if it rains?' he asked Sarah, taking a moment to be practical.

'Retractable roofs and screens. We monitor the weather pretty closely, and if there's a chance of rain we come down and secure the platforms. Tonight is clear, though,' Sarah said. 'Cool, but no rain.'

'Excellent,' Finn replied. He turned to look at Callie, who was looking at the tree house in horror. 'Callie…?'

'My room is up *there*?' she whispered, staring at the huge tree.

Oh, so this wasn't what she was expecting. Finn hoped that she wouldn't make a scene—not on their first night. Besides, thousands of people all over the world would give their right arm and a considerable portion of their bank account to sleep under the stars in a luxury tree house on an African game reserve.

'Problem, honey?'

Out of the corner of his eye he could see Sarah stiffening, her welcoming face turning wary. *Please don't turn out to be a city girl diva, Callie,* he silently begged her.

'Look, I think the idea of sleeping in a tree house is seriously wonderful, but—well, this is a game reserve, right? And game reserves have wild animals. And some of those animals—like leopards—like to climb trees! I do *not* want to be a leopard's breakfast!' Callie stated, with a touch of hysteria in her voice.

Sarah bit the inside of her lip to keep from smiling. 'The tree house is completely animal-proof, Mrs Banning.'

Whoah—*Mrs Banning.* That sounded weird.

But Callie didn't seem particularly fazed about what she was being called. She was still fixating on ending up on the local leopard's menu. 'You're sure?'

'Very. We would never put our guests at risk,' Sarah assured her. 'Obviously we ask you to confine your movements to the platforms. If you do so, you'll be absolutely safe. And I'll leave you with a radio and a mobile phone to call me if there is any problem at all.'

A hyena barked in the distance and Callie jumped.

Sarah looked around. 'That being said, I'd prefer that we get you into the tree house. It's not safe to hang around in the bush.'

Callie practically scampered off the seat to stand between Sarah and Finn. Finn took her cold hand in his and linked their fingers together. Sarah walked around to the back of the Land Rover and looked at their pile of luggage. Well, Callie's pile of luggage. He just had one suitcase.

'Let me see you inside and then I'll come back for the luggage.'

Finn shook his head. 'Nah, I'll help. Cal, do you need all these suitcases or can you get away with just one?'

Callie pointed to the smaller case and her tote bag. 'I just need those two.'

Sarah looked relieved as she reached for Callie's bag.

Finn leaned past her and snagged his suitcase and Callie's tote bag. 'I've got it,' he told Sarah, who had started to protest.

'I'll store your other bags at the lodge, Mrs Banning.'

Mrs Banning. Still weird.

'We've set out a picnic dinner for you, including some wine and beer. There is also a selection of spirits and mixers. If you are unhappy with our selection please just call Reception and we'll have someone deliver anything you require,' Sarah said as she led them to the tree house.

As they walked up the stairs Sarah secured a gate behind them, and Finn could see the unobtrusive but strong netting under the first platform that would prevent leopards or any other creatures from making a nocturnal visit. He pointed out the animal-proofing to Callie and watched her shoulders drop a half-inch. He allowed himself a small grin as Sarah showed them the facilities, which included a shower, his and hers basins, and a slipper bath on the edge of the platform that overlooked the river and the valley below.

The second floor held comfortable couches and chairs, a hammock strung between two branches, and a small dining table covered with cloche dishes and champagne bottles in ice buckets. There was a small chest freezer containing soft drinks and beer, and a steel wine rack holding five bottles of exceptional red wine.

How much did they expect them to drink in one night? Finn wondered.

'I'll leave you to explore the bedroom on your own,' Sarah told him, gesturing to the mobile and the radio on a side table. 'You'll hear lions and hyenas, typical bush noises, but do not hesitate to radio or call me if you are uncomfortable or encounter a problem. Nick will collect you at six a.m. for a guided tour—which is a pretty big deal because he rarely does them any more.'

'Why not?' Callie asked.

'Pretty wife in his bed…' Finn explained, and was enchanted by her blush.

'Also the fact that he has two kids under the age of three who are up and roaring around at that time,' Sarah added, before bidding them goodnight and leaving them to their night under the African stars.

Within minutes they heard the Land Rover pulling away and Finn turned to Callie and gestured to the view. 'So, what do you think?'

'Pretty shoddy digs…' Callie teased. 'They've gone to absolutely no trouble at all.'

Finn watched as she walked to the edge of the platform and placed her hands on the safety railing. 'Want some champagne?'

Callie looked at him over her shoulder and wrinkled her nose. 'No, thanks. Actually, I'd love a beer.'

Finn poured beer into a glass for her and brought it and his own bottle over to where she stood. In silence they scanned the river, saw a pod of hippos on the far bank, and watched as the sun tossed ribbons of gold over the treetops.

Finn saw her shiver as the temperature dropped further and allowed the backs of his fingers to drift over the bare skin of her shoulders. 'You're cold… This wind has a bite to it. Why don't you change into something warm and I'll start a fire in the pit?'

Callie looked around. 'Where are our bags?'

'Sarah took them to the bedroom area,' Finn replied.

'Ah, the bedroom area. Bet you it's a massive bed covered in white linen and a mosquito net, surrounded by candles.'

'That's a sucker bet,' Finn replied.

Callie took a nervous sip of her beer before lifting her eyes to Finn's. 'So, are we still paying it by ear?'

He'd never met a woman as direct as Callie before. He liked that—respected it. He didn't need to play games with her.

But she wasn't ready to share herself with him yet, Finn realised. He could see reluctance in the hitch of her shoulders, the slight shake of her fingers—although that might be from the cold—and in the worry in her eyes. She would share his bed one of these days—just not yet. And that was okay. He could wait until the time was right.

And, in the spirit of honesty, he knew the more time he had between his break-up and sleeping with her, the better handle he'd have on this entire situation. *Damn*, it would all be so much easier if he didn't like her quite so much—and if she didn't make his junk want to do a happy dance whenever she breathed.

So. Much. Easier.

Finn's expression turned serious. 'I have the sense that your flirty nature doesn't often translate into bedtime fun.'

Callie tipped her head. 'How do you figure?'

'Well, if it meant less to you then we'd have already ripped each other's clothes off.'

Callie looked out at the stygian darkness. 'It wasn't always like that. I was a lot more impetuous when I was younger.' She held up her hand to explain. 'I wasn't a slut—I just didn't take sex as seriously as I do now. It used to just be a romp...some slap and tickle...fun...'

'It still can be,' Finn said, his eyes locked on her face.

'I know, but these days I prefer to have a little bit of friendship with my sex. Just a smidgeon—I don't expect more than that—but liking is a prerequisite, respect is a bonus.'

'I like you.'

'I like you too, but…'

Finn quirked an eyebrow. 'But?'

'But…' Callie sighed. 'I'm just not—'

Callie stopped speaking and Finn waited for her to finish her thought. She just wasn't *what*?

Callie sighed. 'Ready. I'm just not ready.'

Yeah, and that was a lie. There was another reason why she was hesitating, why she was treading carefully. She wanted him—he knew that…had no doubts about that. So something else was causing her to hesitate. What was it and why was he so desperate to know?

Callie was waiting for his reply, buy there was nothing that he could say except, 'We won't be doing anything together until you are a hundred per cent comfortable with me, Cal. So try and relax, stop worrying, go and get warm. We can share a bed without me jumping you, I promise. Actually, tonight I'd love to sleep in this hammock. It looks super-comfortable and I've slept in far worse.' Finn took a long sip of his beer. 'Go and put something warm on, honey.'

Callie nodded, put her untouched beer on the table and walked to the stairs leading to the sleeping platform. Finn watched her gorgeous ass moving up the spiral staircase and felt the action in his pants.

All he had to do was follow her, start kissing her, and she'd be his. He knew that. God, it was tempting. But he didn't want to have to coerce her, tempt her, persuade her. When they made love it would be because it was a mutual decision.

It had something to do with the respect that Callie had been talking about earlier.

'Finn! This bedroom is *amazing*!' Callie called down

to him. 'Come up here and look at this place. It would be like having sex in the clouds—I mean, sleeping with you in the clouds—I mean... *Aaarrrgggh!* Dammit!'

Finn grinned, happy that he wasn't the only one who had his mind in the bedroom.

'Ignore me.' Callie's low voice drifted down to him.

Yeah, not easy to do, Finn silently assured her as he swallowed his chuckle.

Callie pushed her plate away and groaned as she leaned back in her chair. She'd expected a cold supper. She hadn't expected delicious prawns, spicy fish fillets and perfectly cooked steak. There'd also been a couscous salad and a watermelon, olive and feta salad, along with crusty bread and a variety of dips.

After the flight from Cape Town and two glasses of red wine she was feeling lazy and hazy and very sleepy. At nearly eight it was fully dark, and the soundtrack of the African bush had started to play. The crickets chirping was a familiar sound, and there was the power saw noise of the African cicada beetle. Occasionally a fish eagle would let rip with a *heee-ah, heeah-heeah*, and from somewhere that sounded far too close they heard the yelping, woofing and whining of what Finn said was a family of black-backed jackals.

It was noisy, Callie realised. *Very* noisy.

Finn, his strong features looking even more handsome in the low light of the paraffin lamps, looked at her across the table. 'There's chocolate mousse in the cool box.'

'I wish I could. I'm stuffed.'

Like her, Finn had pulled on jeans and a hooded sweatshirt against the cool night air. The blazing fire in the pit kept the worst of the chill off, but this was a place that invited you to have a warm shower and then to snuggle under the down duvet on the bed upstairs, warm in each other's arms.

It was an attractive proposition, Callie thought. But Finn had reiterated his wish to sleep in the double hammock. He'd found another down duvet in a storage cupboard on the bathroom platform and announced that he'd be super-warm wrapped up in it in the hammock.

'You look tired,' Finn commentated, lifting his glass of red to his lips.

'I am.' Callie leaned her arms on the table. 'It's been an interesting week.'

'You should've been in Paris by now.'

Tearing around the city, rushing from designer to designer, not having a moment to enjoy the city in the spring... Callie thought that she would much rather be here.

'You never told me what happened that you could suddenly take me up on my offer to be a fake wife.'

Could she tell him? Would he understand? Callie ran her finger around the rim of her full glass. He was treating her to three weeks in luxury—maybe he deserved an explanation. And, geez, they were going to be in each other's company for three weeks—they were going to *have* to talk! They were going to be friends whether they liked it or not. It was up to her to keep things casual.

'I'm running away—trying to avoid someone,' she said, looking into the fire pit. So much for keeping it casual!

'Yeah, I sort of realised that.' Finn stretched out his legs and rested his wine glass on his folded arm. 'So, who is Laura and why are you avoiding her?'

Callie jerked her head up. 'Where did you hear that name?'

'The other day, when you were arguing with your brother. Who is she?' Finn asked again.

Well, she'd started this conversation, she couldn't shut it down now.

'My mother,' Callie said, slouching down in her chair, crossing her feet at the ankles. 'She left us. We haven't heard from her since I was seven. Seb, my brother, has been tracking her movements around the world for years—he's a hacker and can do that—and they started exchanging emails. The result of which is that Laura is coming home for a three-week visit, landing—' Callie checked her watch '—in about an hour. She and Seb are going to reconnect, and everybody wants me to meet her too. Well, "everybody" being Seb.'

'And you made damn sure that there was no possibility of that happening by leaving the city with me? That's why you changed your mind about coming?' Finn said, his voice deep in the darkness.

'Yeah. I needed to leave and you gave me a damn good excuse.' Would he think she was a coward? That she was being immature? Why did it matter so much that he didn't judge her?

Finn pulled his legs in and sat up. 'So why don't you want to meet her? Why don't you want to hear why she left?'

That question again, Callie thought.

'Because it doesn't matter! Because nothing she can say—and, trust me, I've thought of every excuse she could come up with—would make me feel better, would make me understand. I was *seven*, Finn. Seven! I needed a mother. Especially since my dad dealt with my mother leaving by hooking up with younger and younger women. They were mostly after his money, and weren't interested in his little daughter hanging around. Seb was twelve, and he dealt with her leaving by withdrawing into his sports and computers.'

Callie heard her voice rise and made a conscious effort to remain calm.

'If it wasn't for Rowan, who lived next door, and Yasmeen—'

'Who is she?'

'Our housekeeper—and I suppose my real mother in every way that counted,' Callie explained. She pushed her hair off her forehead and shoulders. 'Look, I know I sound harsh, but I can't meet Laura. I don't want to...'

'Don't want to meet her, like her, risk being hurt by her again?'

'Yeah.'

He got it—he understood. *Damn.* There were those fuzzies in her tummy again. She could get used to those. *Not* a good idea.

Finn rested his forearms on his thighs and looked up at her, sparks from the fire reflected in his eyes. Callie, feeling as if he'd taken a peek into part of her soul, thought that he'd heard enough from her, so she turned the spotlight onto him.

'So, you mentioned your stepbrothers? How many do you have?'

Finn half smiled. 'Three. All younger. They're driving me nuts lately.'

'Why?'

'They were, to put it mildly, upset that the wedding was called off. As I said, because they know me, and know that I never go back on my word, they assumed that the break-up was Liz's idea. I haven't bought food for two weeks because someone always pitches up at my house with beer and take-out.'

'Nobody rocked up that night I had dinner at your house,' Callie pointed out.

'I sent them a group message while I was upstairs and told them I would kick their ass if they didn't give me a night on my own.' Finn pulled a face. 'The next night I had all three of them coming to check up on me and had to spend half the evening reassuring them that I was okay.'

'And are you?' Callie asked. 'Okay?'

'Mostly. I'm glad to still be on this assignment, working. Glad of the distraction that is you.'

Callie smiled at that. Whatever they had cooking it was, she had to admit, a hell of a distraction. 'It's surprising that your younger brothers are so protective of you.'

'We're protective of each other. They're my brothers. My mum married James when I was fourteen and he already had the boys. Mum died when I was seventeen, and James acted as my legal guardian for a while.'

'Where's your real dad?'

'Who the hell knows? Jail? Dead? In a gutter somewhere?' Finn said harshly.

He rubbed a hand over his face, and when he finally met her eyes she made sure that her face was impassive.

'Pretend I didn't say that, please? I never talk about him and I have no idea where that came from.'

Maybe their bottle of wine had contained some magic truth potion, because she'd had no intention of telling him about Laura. Or maybe it was the fact that they were absolutely, utterly alone under an African night sky...

Or maybe it was because they liked talking to each other.

And she thought that *she* had had a messed-up childhood. God, they were a pair, Callie thought.

Finn cleared his throat before speaking again. 'I've always protected my brothers—yanked them out of scrapes, had their back. I've been their rock, their calm in the storm. This break-up has been the first crisis I've had that they've witnessed and they want to be there for me.'

'And your stepdad? How does he feel about your break-up?'

Finn shrugged and kept his shoulders up around his ears. 'Dunno. He died about six months ago.'

'I'm so sorry, Finn. You two were close?'

'Yeah. He was the best man I ever knew...' Finn cleared his throat. 'I adored him.'

God. He had a waste-of-space father, a dead mother, and his stepdad, whom he'd loved, had recently passed away. He'd broken up with his fiancée two weeks before his wedding. Was there anything else that life could throw at the poor guy?

Enough now, she told the universe, annoyed on his behalf. *Seriously. Just enough, already.*

Callie leaned forward and touched his knee in silent support. He hadn't stopped grieving, she realised. Probably wouldn't for a while. Losing his fiancée had undoubtedly pulled all those old feelings of grief over losing his stepfather to the surface again.

Oh, yeah, there was far too much emotion swirling around for them to sleep together. Because there was no chance that sex would be about just sex after a conversation like this. For her it would all be tangled up with the urge to soothe, to comfort. And to him she would be just a distraction...

Thinking that it would be prudent, and smart, to close this conversation down, Callie pushed her chair back and stood up. 'I'd really like a shower. I feel grubby.'

Finn stared up at her for the longest time before lifting one broad shoulder. 'Sure.'

Callie looked at the stairs that led to the dark bathroom area below them and bit her lip. 'Is there a torch anywhere?'

Finn stood up. 'I'll go down and light some lamps for you. There's a big tub on the deck if you'd prefer a bath.'

A hyena whooped in the distance and Callie shivered. 'Not that brave. I'm not entirely sure if my standards of animal-proof are the same as the lodge's, so I'd rather not take the chance.'

'The bath is at least twenty foot off the ground, Hollis,' Finn told her, smiling.

'There might a genius leopard out there who has the situation sussed,' Callie suggested, only half joking.

'You're a nut,' Finn said with on a shake of his head and a grin. 'Go get your PJs while I sort out some light for you.'

'Thanks.' Callie bit her bottom lip. 'I don't suppose you'll stand guard, will you?'

Finn touched her bottom lip with the pad of his thumb. 'The only way that will happen is if I'm in the shower with you.' Finn dropped his thumb when she shook her head. 'No, I didn't think so.'

Snuggled down in the enormous bed on the top platform, Callie couldn't keep her eyes off the magnificent night sky. It looked as if God had taken a handful of diamonds and tossed them against a sticky backdrop, allowing them to hang there in a perpetual grip. She'd never seen stars like this before—she almost felt she could reach out and touch them.

She was beyond tired, Callie thought, and wished that sleep would come. But every time she closed her eyes she was jolted by another strange sound. The rustle of something in the tree—probably just the breeze, or a bird—had her constantly on edge. It was *not* the genius leopard, she kept telling herself. And just when she felt her eyelids starting to close those pesky jackals would start their yelping again, and then something would grunt and the hyena would laugh.

Callie was over her night under the African stars and was not finding anything remotely amusing. She was exhausted, slightly chilled, and—though she hated to admit it—a lot scared. She realised she *liked* having walls and windows between her and the night, locks and safety chains. She didn't like feeling as if she was a snack on the buffet of the African savannah, and it didn't matter how much Mr Cool downstairs reassured her: this was *not* natural! Or maybe it was *too* natural.

Again—walls, doors, windows! That was what God had created them for!

The sounds of the night dropped away and Callie felt her eyelids drooping. She was on that wonderful edge of sleep when she felt a rumbling in her chest, felt electricity charge the air. Instantly the night sounds ceased as a deep-throated grunt echoed across the bush. Oh, crap!

Callie scrambled up in bed and pulled the duvet over her head.

The grunt increased in intensity and she felt the sound invade her chest, skitter down to her nerve-endings. *Lion!* Callie sucked in her breath and wished that she could belt out of bed and run all the way back to Cape Town. The deep grunts tailed off and she bit her lip, waiting for the next sound. Just when she thought that the lion had stopped he let out a massive, deep-throated roar that raised every hair on her arms.

God—oh, God—oh, God. Finn had to call the lodge. There was a lion below them. Who could sleep with a lion below them?

'Finn!' she whispered.

Finn didn't reply.

Throwing back the covers, Callie grabbed all her courage and belted for the stairs. She cursed when she stubbed her big toe against a table. The roars were still reverberating through the night. In bare feet she scampered down the steps and by sheer chance located the radio and mobile on the table, where Sarah had left them. Her shaky hands fumbled with the unfamiliar device.

'Whatcha doing?' Finn's drowsy voice came from the direction of the hammock.

'Finn! There's a lion below us!' Callie hissed. 'We've got to call the lodge!'

'Um, okay. Why?'

'Because there's a *lion*!' Callie shouted. 'Below us!'

'Lions don't climb trees, Hollis, especially animal-proofed trees,' Finn drawled.

If she hadn't been so freaked out Callie would have heard the amusement in his voice.

Another roar rolled through the stygian darkness and Callie jumped, dropping the mobile which skittered away. She swore and peered down at the pitch-black floor. She couldn't see the phone so she swore again.

She was going to owe Rowan a lot of money after to-night.

'Cal, calm down, honey.' Finn's voice was low and steady, a beacon in the darkness. 'Leave the phone and head over here.'

Thinking that sounded like a very good plan, Callie inched her way over the deck to the bulky outline that was Finn lying in the hammock. When she stood next to him he lifted his hands and in one smooth movement lifted her, so that she lay on top of him. Rolling her off, he pulled the duvet out from under her and pulled her up so that her head rested on his shoulder.

'Uh...what are you doing?'

'Trying to get you to settle down so that we both can get some sleep,' he muttered.

His hand rested on her lower back and she snuggled up to his warmth.

'Now, listen to me, city girl. A lion's roar can be heard up to five miles away, and I promise you that lion is no-where near us. Yeah, he sounds amazing, but he's not about to eat us—so calm down, okay?'

'I still think we should call the lodge,' Callie protested on a huge yawn.

'What would we tell them? A lion is roaring? *Yeah, that's what they do in the wild, Mr Banning.* They'll think that I have the tiniest pair of balls in creation,' Finn scoffed.

'I'll call them and tell them that *you* aren't scared but I am terrified.'

Finn's sigh brushed the top of her head. 'There's nothing to be frightened of. Listen. He's stopped.'

Callie lifted her head and, true enough, the grunts and roars had stopped. She was just starting to relax when another rumbling loud roar split the night. Callie yelped and buried her face in Finn's neck, plastered herself tightly against him, hoping to climb inside.

Finn sighed. 'Or maybe not.'

Finn's hand stroked her neck, her hair, her back. His voice was low and warm and calming. 'You're safe, Cal, I promise.'

Callie shivered in his arms.

'Breathe, angel,' he told her.

Callie pulled in long deep breaths, felt his warmth and his strength and breathed again. Then her eyelids started to close and she pulled in another deep breath.

In Finn's arms, fast asleep, feeling warm and safe, she didn't even hear the next roar that shattered the night.

CHAPTER SEVEN

THEY DINED OUTSIDE the following evening, at a beautifully laid table on the lawn of the lodge, under another magnificent star-heavy sky. In the distance they could see a storm, the lightning lighting up huge thunderclouds. They could taste the rain in the air but were assured that dinner would be long over before the storm hit, so they sat back to enjoy the exceptional food placed in front of them.

Finn noticed that the lead singer of a popular band sat with a pouty waif at the next table, and beyond them he recognised an English politician with a woman who was definitely not his wife. If he were a tabloid journalist he would be having a field-day right now; he might be feeling a bit sleazy but he'd be making a fortune, he thought.

He looked across at Callie, who was leaning back in her chair, holding her wine glass, her eyes fixed on the storm on the horizon. God, she was beautiful, he thought. He'd always thought that she was attractive, but now, after seeing her without make-up and dozy with sleep, or animated and thrilled while she bottle-fed two orphaned cheetah cubs, or pensive while watching a pride of lions take down a zebra, he was slowly realising that she was more than pretty and deeper than he'd thought.

He'd thought that he would be taking a bubbly flirt on holiday with him, but the woman he was with—even if he'd only spent two full days in her company—was less bubble, more substance. And sexier than he'd believed possible.

Finn dropped his hand and surreptitiously rearranged himself under the table, feeling as if his pants were suddenly a size too small. Since he'd woken up with her clinging to him like an octopus he'd been super-aware of her all day. The length of her legs, the freckles on her chest, her white-tipped fingernails. God, if he was noticing a woman's nails then he was in deep, *deep* crap.

He'd thought he was going on holiday with Flirty Callie but instead he found himself with Intriguing Callie, and he wasn't sure he could handle her. Flirty Callie he could brush off—ignore if he had to. This other Callie had him wanting to dig a little, to see what was below the surface.

Finn took a sip of his Cabernet and pushed his dessert plate away. Then he manoeuvred his chair so that he was sitting next to her, facing the storm. He could smell her perfume and feel the heat of her bare shoulder when he touched it with his.

He slid his hand under hers and linked her fingers with his. He saw the quick, searching look she sent him and ignored it. If she asked he'd say that this was what married people did—touched each other—but the truth was that he couldn't sit there and *not* touch her.

'Tell me about your jewellery box.'

There was so much else he wanted to know about her—he had a list of burning questions—but this topic seemed the safest, the most innocuous.

He heard her quick intake of breath, felt her eyes on his face.

He slowly turned his head and lifted his eyebrows. 'Why would a woman who loves clothes and shoes and accessories not wear some of that fabulous jewellery?'

Callie crossed one leg over the other and her swinging foot told him she was considering her response, choosing her words. He didn't want the bog standard answer she obviously wanted to hand him—he wanted the truth. He'd rather not know than have her spin him a line.

'Don't wrap the truth up in a pretty bow—give it to me straight.'

The foot stopped swinging and the sigh was louder this time. She took so long to say anything that Finn began to doubt that she would speak at all. When she did, her voice was low and tight with tension.

'That was the first time I'd seen the box for...oh, fifteen years. It lived on my mum's dressing table and as a little girl I'd spend hours playing with her bangles and necklaces. Her rings.'

Finn tried not to wince at the thought of little Callie playing with the two and three carat diamonds he'd seen.

'Some of the jewellery was my grandmother's—my father's mother's—passed down through the family. A lot of it is my mother's. My father constantly bought her jewellery in an attempt to make her happy.'

Ah, well... 'I take it that the buying of jewellery didn't work?'

'Not so much. Neither did the pretty clothes and the gym membership and the credit cards.' Callie shrugged. 'She didn't want to be a wife...a mother. To be chained to my dad, the house, us. She gave birth to the expected son and was horrified, I once heard, to find herself pregnant with me. She'd never really wanted children, and apparently finding herself pregnant with me was a disaster of magnificent proportions.'

'Who told you that?'

Callie crossed her legs and shuffled in her chair. 'People say that kids don't remember stuff, but I do. She screamed that during one of their fights.'

'I'm sorry.' It was all he could say—all he could think of to say. Finn removed his hand from hers and put his arm around her shoulder, leaning sideways to kiss her temple. 'But people do say stuff they don't mean in the heat of the moment.'

'Except that her leaving me—us—made that statement true.' Callie took a large, serious sip from her glass. 'Anyway, the jewellery—she left it behind. It meant nothing to her. So why should it mean anything to me?'

God. Imagine knowing that your mother was out there somewhere but not interested in knowing whether you were dead or alive, happy or sad. People should have to take a test before they were allowed to become parents, Finn thought. His father should head up the queue.

Callie turned her head and blinded him with a big smile, perfect teeth flashing. 'Now, don't you go all sympathetic on me, Banning. I had a father who adored me and spoilt me rotten, an older brother who adored me and spoilt me rotten, and a housekeeper-cum-nanny who—'

'Let me guess,' Finn interrupted, making sure that his tone was bone-dry. 'Who adored you and spoilt you rotten?'

Callie laughed. 'I have a fabulous life, and I'm on holiday with a nice man.'

'I prefer sexy.'

This time her smile was more genuine. 'So I have nothing to complain about!'

Being abandoned by your mum is a pretty big deal, Callie, Finn told her silently. *Even if you choose to think it isn't. The one person who is supposed to put you first, love you best, stand in your corner left you. That's got to cause some deep scars on your psyche.*

Feeling the need to banish the sadness from her eyes, Finn nudged her with his shoulder. 'Want to take a walk down to the lookout over the waterhole and see if any wildlife has come down for a drink?'

Callie immediately nodded and a sparkle returned to

her eyes. 'Yeah, let's do that.' She stood up and folded her arms. 'How come I find myself telling you stuff?'

Finn wanted to make a joke but he couldn't. 'I don't know, but rest assured you're not alone. I keep doing the same thing.'

Callie bit her lip. 'Maybe we should stop?'

Finn held out his hand. 'Yeah, maybe we should. The thing is, I don't know if we can.'

There was nobody in the lookout and nothing at the waterhole except for a lone bull elephant. They watched him and the storm for a while, but Callie's thoughts were miles away. On Finn and their bizarre situation, and on the fact that every time they drew a line in the sand they managed either to smudge it or step right over it.

Maybe it was time to draw a line that couldn't be removed, stepped over or just plain ignored. But how to do that?

Callie yawned and felt his arm come around her shoulders. Without thought she circled her arms around his trim waist and laid her cheek on his chest.

Smudging that line again, Hollis?

Callie felt Finn's kiss on her hair. 'Tired?'

'Mmm…'

Callie moved her hands to his abs and Finn sucked in his breath. In response she scraped her nails across his cotton-covered skin. A quick glance down and she realised, by the tenting of his pants, that he had a hair trigger response to her touch.

This wasn't smudging the line—this was obliterating it. Was she prepared to go there? She had about five seconds either to take this to the next level or to back away.

Callie knew herself well enough to know that she wasn't going to step away. She was facing a fire and for the first time in, God, so long she was going to jump right in. But this time she was going to be a little wiser and don a fire suit.

'Finn?'

'Yeah?' His voice was husky with desire and so sexy.

'That thing that happened in the dressing room...I keep thinking about it.'

She knew exactly when he stopped breathing, when he finally sucked in much needed air. 'Okay. Where are you going with this?'

'Our room only has one bed, and if I climb into it with you I'm going to be all over you.'

Callie forced herself to walk out of his grip, to pick up the bottle of beer he'd brought with him and take the last sip. To keep herself from jumping him, she held the bottle in a loose grip.

Finn groaned. 'Good to know. Want to get going, then?'

She smiled at the hopeful note in his voice before quietly murmuring, 'Holiday romances seldom work out.'

'That's what I've heard.'

'People tend to put on rose-coloured glasses and, because they know their time together is short, the experience can be intense, powerful.'

'I guess.'

Callie rolled the bottle between her palms. 'I'm at a bit of a crossroads in my life and I'm questioning so much. I'm not thinking as straight as I usually do, so don't let me get forget that this is a couple of weeks of pure fun, okay? Don't let me get seduced by the luxury and the romance and the fact that I like you.'

That was the line in the sand, she decided. They could chat and talk, share confidences and make incredible love, but she had to remember that this was going to end. It was too easy to forget who they were and why they were here. It was not real life. They were on a fake honeymoon—emphasis on the *fake*—surrounded by romance and luxury.

She could easily get swept away and inadvertently slip on a pair of those rose-coloured glasses.

They were two strangers who hardly knew each other—not a couple on their honeymoon. They could have fun, even sex, but they had to keep it real. She wasn't in a place to consider a relationship beyond the three weeks. Sure, it would be easy to fall for Finn, but it wouldn't last because it wasn't based on anything real.

She—*they*—had to keep their eyes open, their heads in the game. If she had sex with him she would finally know how he felt, tasted, moved. and then she could stop thinking about him—and sex—all the damn time.

Callie turned her head and sent him a direct look. 'We're on the same page?'

He rubbed his hand over his jaw before nodding briskly. 'Yeah. Just to be clear, are you saying that you'll sleep with me?'

The tip of her tongue touched her top lip and her skin flushed with anticipated pleasure. *Yeah, that was the plan.* Callie held his eyes.

'Well, sleep isn't what we'll be doing, exactly.' He made a move towards her but her lifted hand stopped him in his tracks. 'I don't want to be seduced, Finn.'

She saw a moment of confusion and then his face cleared. 'No hearts and flowers, no expectations.'

How did he seem to know without her having to explain? It was unsettling, but reassuring at the same time.

Finn touched her bottom lip with the pad of his thumb. 'Only in my bed, honey. I promise. Sex is on the table—everything else is off it.'

They could do this, Callie thought as they made their way out of the hide and across the lawns to their new room behind the main lodge. If they were smart and sensible, and if they kept their heads, they could have three weeks of fun and walk away unscathed.

They *had* to do this, Callie amended as Finn took her hand in his. They didn't have another option.

In their private chalet within the protected grounds of the lodge Finn took her hand and led her out onto a dark, private veranda, where moonlight glistened off the bubbles created by the hot tub that sat in one corner. Callie watched his face as he reached behind her and slid down the zip of her simple A-line dress, pulling the collar away from her neck and allowing the silky sage-green fabric to fall to the wooden deck. She stood in her violet strapless bra and matching panties, open to his appreciative gaze, watching his eyes as one index finger traced her collarbone, her shoulder, the top of her right breast.

He looked entranced, engrossed, fully involved in touching her, learning her shape, making her a memory. *Don't get fanciful,* she warned herself, closing her eyes as his finger touched her nipple and it tightened and peaked immediately.

'This is about sex, about pleasure, about a three-week affair,' Callie gabbled, closing her eyes at the intense pleasure his touch aroused in her.

'Shut up, Callie,' Finn murmured gently.

You've had these before, remember? she told herself. *You sleep with him until it stops being fun and then you stop. It's not rocket science.*

Except that Finn touching her didn't feel like just another sex act, just another pursuit of physical pleasure. It felt like something more. Deeper, more important.

Finn's mouth brushed her ear. 'Stop thinking,' he muttered. 'Just feel me touching you, enjoying your smooth skin, tasting you, smelling you. You do the same to me.'

His breath tickled her cheek and the touch of his finger on her skin had heat pooling between her thighs, causing a rush of moisture to her panties. He had barely even started and she was already ready for him to take her—*right now*. Oh, this was going to be amazing, incredible...

'I think you should kiss me,' Callie said against his cheekbone.

'I think I'll go up like a cracker,' was Finn's wry reply.

Callie dropped her gaze to his pants and sucked in her breath. Unable to stop herself, she ran her finger down the long, rock-hard length of him.

Finn grabbed her wrist and pulled her hand away. 'Yeah, also not a good idea.'

'I need you to—'

'Honey, I know exactly what you need.' Finn lifted his hand and tipped her chin up. Their eyes slammed together and held. 'Trust me to take care of you.'

'I do...'

'You sure?'

'If you can make me forget who I am in a semi-public dressing room, I have no doubt that you can do it now.'

Finn waited a beat before he shot his arm out, encircled her hips and slammed her into him. As her mound made contact with his erection his tongue swept into her mouth. He tasted and tormented her, swirling her away on a whirlpool of pleasure. His hand slid into the back of her panties and he palmed her butt with his broad hands, dipping lower, stretching the silk over his wrists so that he could touch her inner thighs and explore her feminine folds.

Callie shuddered as she fumbled for the buttons on his shirt, ripping off the last one in her haste to feel his broad chest and his hard, ribbed stomach.

'Want you...want you...want you...' she chanted, standing on her tiptoes to nibble his jaw, to swirl her tongue down his neck.

Finn pulled his hands out from her panties and with one deft flick her bra fell between them. Callie couldn't have cared less; her nipples were rubbing through the hair on his chest and if he didn't touch her soon, in all those important burning places, she was going to scream.

Loudly.

Unable to wait, she took one of Finn's hands and placed it on her breast, tried to direct his other hand to her crotch. But instead of taking her direction Finn stepped away from her and shook his head.

'No—you're saying *no*?' Callie cried, her fists on her hips. She couldn't believe that he was stepping away, that he was backing off.

Finn had the audacity to laugh at her before his eyes turned serious. 'I have a feeling that you normally call the shots in the bedroom, but this time—this first time—I'm running the show, angel.'

His thumb rubbed her cheekbone and she forgot her thought.

'You said that you trusted me. Take your panties off.'

Callie looked at him, her mouth drying at his command. She was always in the driving seat when it came to sex—she set the pace—and it felt strange and wildly intoxicating to relinquish control. Her heart was pumping at a mile a minute.

She licked her lips before hooking her thumbs in the band of her panties and shimmying them over her hips. Finn looked at her lightning-shaped strip of pubic hair and his lips twitched. When he lifted his eyes again the humour had been replaced by flat-out desire.

'That's new.'

'Shut up...' Callie growled. They could discuss her beautician's creative streak later.

'Go and sit on the edge of the hot tub—feet in the water, legs open.'

Callie turned her back to him, walked up the steps to the tub and stepped over the ledge, dropping her feet into the hot, gorgeous water. She sighed her pleasure and couldn't help wondering what was coming next.

'Yeah, keep your eyes closed,' Finn told her. 'This is about you—only you.'

God, could she stand it? Callie thought as she obeyed his instruction. Immediately her other senses were heightened: she could taste the approaching storm on her lips, could smell the citronella in the candles that she heard Finn lighting, could feel bubbles popping against her feet and her calves.

The crickets were in full chorus again, and she thought she heard the bark of a zebra.

Callie had no idea where Finn was. She had heard the rustle of his clothing as he undressed, but after that nothing more. He'd gone Ninja on her, but she couldn't open her eyes—not until he told her to.

'Open your legs, Cal.'

Callie shivered as his voice caressed her skin, causing goosebumps up and down her arms. 'Wider, honey. Yeah. So pretty. No, don't open your eyes. Let me look at you.'

Callie sat on the edge of the tub, her eyes closed, feeling wild and free and as much a part of this savage place as the predators and the prey. Time slowed and the seconds ticked over sluggishly. She was content just to sit there and let her about-to-be lover look at her.

An owl screeched, a candle spluttered, and Callie yelped as hard hands pulled her knees further apart and a dark head appeared between her thighs. Then his mouth, hot, wild and experienced, dropped onto her sex and she bucked against him, her cries blending into the sounds of the night.

Callie gripped the sides of the tub as Finn pleasured her with his lips, his tongue, slid first one finger into her, then two. She arched her back as her orgasm built, desperate for Finn to push her over the edge. But just as she crested he pulled back, and she keened her disappointment. He allowed her to fall, just a little, before building her up again.

He repeated the torture until he lifted his head, looked her straight in the eye and, with his fingers still inside her, issued another order. 'Come for me. *Now*.'

And Callie responded, just as he knew she would, instantly gushing over his hand, her inner muscles gripping his fingers and seeking all the pleasure he could give her. Finn kept his eyes locked on hers, thoroughly captivated by her uninhibited response.

When she finally stopped shaking he pulled his hand away and lifted his arm to grab her waist and pull her into the middle of the tub. She wound her legs around his hips and felt the divine friction as her clit rubbed against his penis, revving her up again. She rode him and felt vindicated, powerful, when his eyes crossed.

Taking him in her fist, she positioned him so that his tip was at her entrance. His bicep bulged with the effort of keeping from ramming himself inside her.

'No condom,' he muttered, his arms shaking.

'I'm on the pill,' she told him. 'And I'm clean. I haven't had sex for over six months and I had a medical three months ago. You?'

'Same. Clean. Trust me?'

Callie didn't bother to reply. She just slid onto him and smiled at his expression, which combined relief with pure, unadulterated pleasure.

'God, you feel so good.'

Finn lifted a wet hand and pushed her hair back from her face. 'You ready to go again?''

'*So* ready.'

He lunged up and into her, his arms a vice around her waist. 'Then hang on, baby.'

Callie managed to push herself away just enough to

look into his eyes. She touched his mouth with the tips of her fingers. 'Finn?'

'Yeah?'

'Come for me. *Now*.'

And, with a roar that was as wild as the bush around them, Finn did exactly as she commanded.

'In the nineteenth century the local tribe in the area knew it as Mosi-oa-Tunya. Translated, that means the smoke that thunders.'

Callie stood gripped the railing in front of her and watched, utterly fascinated, as millions and millions of gallons of water thundered over the edge of the falls into a gorge over one hundred metres below them.

'The Victoria Falls is known as the greatest curtain of falling water in the world,' Finn told her, his face wet from the droplets of spray. 'The spray can be seen from miles away at the height of the rainy season. Apparently more than five hundred million cubic metres of water per minute plummet over the edge, over a width of nearly two kilometres.'

'Thank you, guidebook Finn,' Callie said dryly.

Finn pushed his wet hair off his forehead. 'It *is* an incredible sight, though, isn't it?

'It so is,' Callie agreed.

Finn placed his forearms on the railing and lifted his head to squint up at her. 'I wish we were here in winter,' he said, with a pensive look on his face.

'Why? Apart from the fact that it would be about a hundred degrees cooler than at the height of summer?'

Callie felt as if she was walking around in hot soup and she was melting from the inside out. Africa in late summer, early autumn, was still furnace-hot, she thought. And the towns of Livingstone and Victoria Falls, situated next to the massive river, had killer humidity as well. They were, she'd decided, minutes after landing in Livingstone, Zambia, three hours ago, after a chartered flight from the Baobab and Buffalo, standing above the devil's boiler house.

'Well, in winter, when the water levels are low, you can walk along the lip of the falls. There are rock pools there, and one is called the Devil's Pool.'

That made sense, Callie thought. After stoking the fires of hell, Satan would want to cool down.

Then Finn's words sank in and her eyes widened. 'You can walk across....' she waved at the massive falls behind her '...*that*?'

'Well, there'd be a lot less water.'

'That's insane! People *do* this?' Callie cried, her stomach clenching at the thought.

'Sure. You walk across the rocks, swim through some pools, and then there's this other pool, right at the lip of the falls. The rock lip stops you from going over.'

'And you'd do that?' Callie asked in a squeaky voice.

Finn shrugged. 'Sure. It would be a kick.'

Callie closed her eyes. 'That's insane. It's official: I'm sleeping with a mad man.'

Finn straightened and pushed a long wet strand of hair out of her eyes, tucked it behind her ear. 'Talking of sleeping... This morning was so rushed we haven't had a moment alone for me to ask—are you okay?'

Callie frowned. 'Sure. Why wouldn't I be?'

'You said that it had been a while, and we did it a couple of times last night. You're not sore or tired or—?'

Callie grinned, touched by his concern. She was a little stiff, a little uncomfortable, but she wasn't about to admit that. 'Finn, I'm twenty-eight—not a hundred and eight.'

'Just checkin'.' Finn rubbed his thumb over her cheekbone. 'I had fun.'

Hoo-boy. So had she. 'Me too.'

'Want to do it again?'

Callie made sure that her tone was flippant, carefree. 'Sure—since you're *marginally* good at it.'

She put her tongue in her cheek to make sure that he knew that she was teasing.

In a flash Finn scooped her up into his arms and swung her towards the railing. 'Can you swim?' he asked, grinning down at her.

Callie wound her arms around his neck in a chokehold as she squealed hysterically. 'Put me down, you jerk!'

Finn swung her towards the railing again. 'Tell me I'm the greatest you've ever had.'

'The best ever!' Callie shouted in his ear, tightening her arms. 'I promise!'

Finn finally allowed her legs to drop to the ground, but Callie kept her arms around his neck, peeking out from over his arm. His hands were running up and down her spine.

'You were pretty spectacular yourself, Cal.'

Callie dropped her head back to look into his face. His eyes looked warm and tender, and his mouth—that wonderful mouth—was heading towards hers. She allowed him one brush, two, then a quick taste of her tongue before pulling back and stepping away. Sleeping with him was one thing, but the banter, the teasing, the outright affection had to be curtailed—or at the very least controlled. Or else they'd forget that their fake relationship was...well, fake, and they'd end up in all sorts of emotional trouble.

'I don't want a relationship,' she stated baldly.

He met her eyes. 'Me neither.'

She wanted to tell him that she *really* didn't. She couldn't allow her feelings to be engaged, couldn't hand her heart over and trust its well-being to the hands of another person. As a little girl she'd done that. Her mum had been her entire world and she'd left. Just left.

I can't and won't allow myself to break the habit of a

lifetime and fall for you in any way, shape or form, she told him silently.

She made herself smile at him. 'Just so that you know: I am going to use you and abuse you, then callously toss you aside at the end of three weeks.' *I'm going to treat you like just another short-term prospect...some bed-based fun,* she added silently. *And that means no digging into the past, sharing secrets or stories. It means being sensible and unemotional and playing it super-cool.*

Finn nodded. 'Use, abuse and toss away. Got it.' The corners of his eyes crinkled with laughter. 'You are the most honest woman I've ever met, angel.'

He'd called her that before, and it sounded so natural that she wondered if he even knew he was doing it. Short-term lovers shouldn't have nicknames, but she didn't have the guts to ask him to stop. She rather liked it.

Callie looked down the gorge to the river, to what looked like a tiny speck on the water. Her attention captivated, she leaned forward and immediately felt Finn's hand on her elbow, placed there for protection. She would have to be an idiot to lean far enough over to lose her balance and go headfirst down into the gorge, but Finn's protective instinct warmed her from the inside out.

Don't go there, Hollis. Use, abuse, toss.

'Is that a boat?' Callie asked, pointing to the river so very far below them.

'Yep. That's one of the white-water rafting boats.' Finn nodded. 'I want to do that tomorrow. Want to come with me?'

Callie twisted her lips. 'That would be a no.'

But there was a tug of excitement in her belly—a wish that she could say yes, that she could experience the thrill of riding those rapids. She hadn't done anything to make her adrenalin pound since she was a teenager who'd loved pushing the envelope.

And she wouldn't. She'd promised Seb and her dad. But, *damn*, she'd loved it.

'Aw, come on!' Finn placed a hand on her back to steer her down the path, away from their lookout point.

'You have more chance of being impregnated by a member of the zombie apocalypse.' She leaned her shoulder into his. 'You'd better not die. I'll be narked if my holiday and my recently revived sex life is interrupted by having to ship you home in a body bag.'

Finn grinned at her. 'No worries. It's safe.'

'It's madness!' Callie hissed.

But it wasn't—it really wasn't. It looked fun and exciting and thrilling, and she hoped Finn loved every second of it.

She knew that *she* would. Damn, she could just do it and they wouldn't even know. But she'd promised. And promises couldn't be broken, she reminded herself.

CHAPTER EIGHT

CALLIE, IN A teeny bikini, sat on the deep step of the tepid hotel pool, a virgin mojito by her elbow and her face shielded from the early-afternoon sun by an enormous straw hat. Finn, dressed in a pair of board shorts and holding a beer in his hand, sat next to her, reading a travel magazine.

'I should be working,' he muttered as he flipped a page.

'This *is* working,' Callie assured him. 'You're researching the hotel's facilities.'

Finn didn't lift his eyes from the page. 'I'll go with that. Jeez, what a crock!'

Callie leaned into his shoulder. Judging by the mighty mountains in the photograph, she realised that he was reading an article about the Himalayas.

'What's the problem?'

Finn flicked the magazine with his thumb. 'This journalist is writing about Durbar Square in Kathmandu and being factually incorrect—which annoys the hell out of me. If you're going to write about a foreign place be respectful and get your damn facts straight!'

Callie's lips twitched in amusement. 'I'll keep that in mind if I decide to make a career change.'

'Smart-ass,' Finn muttered, but she saw his quick smile before he refocused on the offending article.

Callie heard her mobile ring She reluctantly stood up

and went to her lounger to answer it. It would be Rowan, or Seb, or her dad calling to check up on her. She could, she thought with a smile, only tell Rowan that she was having fabulous sex…

'I'm fine…I'm happy…I haven't done anything stupid yet,' she said, her voice full of laughter.

'Hello, Calista.'

Callie stiffened and her heart started to pound. She recognised that voice—it was the voice she heard in her dreams. Callie checked the unfamiliar number on her display. 'Who *is* this?' she demanded, although she had no doubt.

'It's your mother.'

Callie shook her head. 'Funny, that—I don't *have* a mother. She left while I was in hospital, getting X-rays for my broken arm and cracked ribs.'

'You always were a challenging child.'

Like you'd know. 'Says the woman who sneaked out through the door and didn't come back.'

'I'm back now.'

'Twenty-plus years too late and I don't care. Who gave you my number? Seb?'

Silence answered that question. 'Tell him he sucks. Don't call me again, Laura, we have nothing to say to each other.'

'Calista—'

Callie pushed the button to disconnect the call and bit down on her lip, concentrating on that pain in an attempt to ignore the throbbing clenching of her heart. Laura sounded exactly the same: her voice low and melodious. She had a beautiful voice, Callie remembered. She'd loved to hear her sing.

God, she couldn't think about her—couldn't start to remember. She didn't want to remember—didn't want to open that Pandora's box. She'd always sung when she was happy...which hadn't been that often.

One phone call and a host of memories flooded back—her laughter, her scent. Callie banded her arms across her stomach, trying to keep the pain at bay. She didn't want to remember, to start thinking about her, about everything she'd lost...

She needed something to distract her—something to make her forget. Callie threw her mobile back into her tote bag and looked to Finn. *He* would make her forget. One touch of his hands on her skin and she would be taken away to a place where no thought was necessary. A place of pleasure and delight...

Callie dived into the pool and surfaced by the step. She tugged on Finn's big toe and when he looked at her lowered her eyelids in a gesture that she hoped was sexy and alluring. 'Want to go back to the cabana and play?' she asked.

Finn pulled his glasses off his face and folded them carefully. He looked at her for a full minute before asking, 'Who called you, Cal?'

Callie pulled in her top lip and shrugged. 'No one important.' Her hand slid up his leg and gripped his knee. 'Let's go and fool around.'

'Nope.'

Callie's mouth fell open in astonishment. The man hadn't been able to keep his hands off her last night and some of this morning and now he was saying *no*? When she most needed him?

'Excuse me?'

Finn held her eyes, his expression inscrutable. 'As tempting as that offer is...no, we're not going back to the room to fool around.'

'Why not?' Callie demanded, finding her feet in the pool.

'Tell me who was on the phone, Cal.'

She didn't want to discuss her mother—that was the point! She didn't want to go there. Didn't want to revisit her bad childhood and her mother issues.

Suddenly she craved the rush of adrenalin, the freedom of doing something extreme, something to get her out of herself. She wanted to be Wild Callie, Free Callie. So if she couldn't have sex in the middle of the day with her fake husband then she'd do something else to get her adrenalin pumping, to distract her.

A part of her knew that she was lapsing back into old childhood habits—as a child and teenager she'd tried every daredevil stunt she could, either to attract attention or to distract herself from her mother-free life. But, God knew, after hearing her mother's voice for the first time in over twenty years, she more than needed a distraction.

Patch and Seb would understand why she had to break her promise.

'Fine.' Callie tossed her head and glared at Finn. 'Then I'm going back to the room, getting dressed, and then I am going to go and bungee jump.'

'Yeah? No. You're not.'

Now he was presuming to tell her what to do? She didn't think so!

'Since I am an adult, and since I am not asking you to pay for it, how do you think you're going to stop me?'

Finn drained the rest of his beer and placed the empty bottle on the side of the pool. He folded his arms and she wished she could crawl into them, rest her head on his chest and allow the tears that she was holding back to slide down her face. But that was impossible. Because Callie Hollis was a tough party-girl. She didn't cry.

'Obviously I can't stop you, if that's what you're determined to do, but yesterday you said that you didn't want to bungee, to do white-water rafting or the microlight over the Falls experience. You said that extreme sports isn't something you do any more.'

'Changed my mind,' Callie retorted.

Please don't sound so concerned and worried. If you do, I might break down totally.

'I can see that. Want to tell me why?'

Callie shook her head. 'I changed my mind. I'm allowed to do that, Finn!'

'Stop treating me like an idiot, Callie! Ten minutes ago you were happy and relaxed and then you got a call. Now you're more wound up than a spinning top! Whoever called you has put you over the edge and now you're acting like a…' Finn's words trailed off.

'A lunatic? A crazy person? A bitch?' Callie asked. God knew she felt like all three. But she didn't owe him an explanation for changing her mind—why couldn't he respect that? She didn't owe anyone anything! Besides, in the past couple of days she'd spoken more about her past than she had in twenty years!

'Now you're putting words in my mouth.'

How was she supposed to fight with him, argue, when he was so calm, so controlled, so unfazed? It was like arguing with a pile of soil—incredibly frustrating.

'Did your mum call you? It was her, wasn't it?'

Oh, God, don't go there, Finn, please. 'I'm not discussing this.'

Finn rested his forearms on his knees and Callie could see the disappointment in his eyes, on his face.

'Okay, Callie, I give up. Go bungee-jumping—do whatever the hell you want.'

'All I wanted to do was make love with you!' Callie cried.

If he'd just said yes, like any normal man, they wouldn't be fighting, wouldn't be having this torturous conversation.

'No, you wanted to use me as a distraction from her call,

from whatever she said, what she made you feel,' Finn replied, his tone low. 'And while I'm happy to have you any time and anywhere, angel, might I remind you that you weren't prepared to be a means for *me* to escape the pain of my break-up? Well, ditto back at you, babe.'

Callie squeezed the rope of wet hair that hung over her shoulder. 'You couldn't even hear what I was saying, so you're jumping to some very big conclusions, Banning!'

Finn tapped his sunglasses against his leg. 'Am I wrong?'

Callie tried to lie—she did—but while her tongue formed the words she couldn't push them past her lips. Unable to hold Finn's stare, she looked up at the deep blue sky before whirling around and plunging back into the pool, allowing her tears to mix with the chlorinated water.

Damn him. All she'd wanted was some crazy sex to help her forget. Was that such a big ask?

Okay, so today had been weird, Finn thought, as he left their room at The Thunder, a small, luxurious boutique hotel situated on the banks of the mighty Zambezi River. He was heading for a huge deck suspended above the river, which offered—according to the pile of literature the manager had left for him to peruse—superb views of wildlife coming down to the river to drink and magnificent sunrises and sunsets.

Right now all he hoped was that it held a certain navy-eyed blonde who was currently avoiding him.

Finn ran his hand through his wet hair before jamming his hands into the pockets of his stone-coloured linen shorts. After their argument she'd swum lengths in the pool, only stopping forty-five minutes later, when her breath was laboured and her limbs were shaking. Her eyes had still been tight with tension, red-rimmed either from the chlorine or her tears, and her lips had been a thin line in her face.

Thinking that he'd pushed her enough, and that she needed some time to cool down, he'd avoided her for the afternoon, taking his laptop and notes and finding a secluded spot in the hotel's library to start work on his honeymoon article.

When he'd surfaced hours later it had been early evening, and when he'd returned to their room Callie's scattered clothes and her light fragrance in the air had told him that she'd already dressed and left for dinner.

She wasn't on the deck, he realised, looking over the tables. Twisting his lips, he walked to the bar area—and there she sat, at the end of the bar, a margarita in her hand, holding court. Two guys his age and an older man were hanging off her every word, tongues practically resting on the bar.

On the other side of the bar Finn leaned his shoulder into the wall and watched her, unnoticed by anyone but the barman. *Look at her,* he thought, *so bold, so attractive, such a fake.* This Callie, this consummate, charming flirt, wasn't who she really was. *All* of who she was.

The real Callie was softer, more vulnerable, a great deal deeper than the person currently charming the pants off her admirers. This woman was harder, phonier, a great deal more Hollywood.

But sexy—always so damn sexy.

The man in him—her lover—got a kick knowing that she would share his bed tonight, be with him tonight. He shrugged. That was his ego talking. It was normal to like the idea of men envying him his woman.

His woman. Wow. Yet for at least the next two weeks she was. Fake wife or not, they were sleeping together, and that allowed him a certain measure of possessiveness. It didn't mean anything serious.

Did it?

Irritated with himself, Finn peeled himself off the wall and walked up to the bar, deliberately placing a hand low on Callie's spine. He felt her stiffen and caught the wary look she tossed his way.

'Evening,' he said, making eye contact with each of her admirers. Being men, and obviously not stupid, they received his non-verbal *back-the-hell-away-from-her* message loud and clear. Within minutes they all had somewhere they needed to be, and he was soon alone with Callie.

He ordered a beer from the barman and looked into her lovely face, immediately clocking her sad eyes, her wariness.

'We still fighting?' he asked gently.

'I was fighting more with you than myself,' she admitted, twisting the wedding ring on her left hand.

'Okay,' Finn replied. He didn't understand, but as long as he was not knee-deep in the brown stuff he was good. 'Do you want to talk about it?'

'Not really.'

He should be happy at that answer, since talking always led them into uncharted, emotional territory, but he couldn't help feeling a little disappointed. He wanted to help her, to work through that brief conversation with her mother that had rocked her world this afternoon.

He was whipped, he decided on an internal sigh. He was feeling protective of her and possessive of her, acting affectionate around her and calling her *angel*. But he felt as if he'd known her for a lot longer than the few weeks he had, and in a sense he seemed to read her better than he ever had Liz. He knew her instinctively.

He was stepping into quicksand and he should back up before he found himself nose-deep in mud and struggling to breathe.

'Okay. The sun is about to go down and I think the sunset is going to be absolutely amazing. Let's go watch it.'

Callie jerked her head in a quick nod and slid off her stool, her long, sleeveless halterneck dress skimming her slim body. The indigo colour lightened her eyes and set off the tan she'd managed to acquire in a few short days. Her naturally curly hair was pulled into a messy plait.

She looked sensational and smelt even better.

Finn picked up her glass and his beer and watched her buttocks sway as she walked towards the open doors and onto the deck. He was pleased when she made her way to a vacant table perched on the end, right over the river and private.

He placed her drink on the table in front of her, pulled out a chair and waited until she was sitting down before settling himself into his own chair. He took a long swig of his beer. He was not going to ask what had gone wrong today.

Finn just sat there, happy to swat mosquitoes away as the sun finger-painted the evening sky with bold oranges and pinks.

A waiter replenished their drinks, brought them a snack of homemade chunky bread and flavoured olive oil to dunk the bread into, and Callie just looked out onto the dark river, her profile exquisite in the low light provided by lamps and citronella candles.

She slapped her bare arm and grimaced at the mess left by a bloodsucking mosquito. 'I'm being eaten alive,' she complained, and he was glad to break the silence—even if it meant discussing the mozzies, which were big enough to pick them up and carry them away.

Which reminded him... 'Did you take your anti-|malaria pill?'

Callie winced. 'Dammit, I forgot.'

Finn shook his head. 'Jeez, Cal, you *can't* forget. Malaria is not fun. Take it when you get back to the room, okay?'

'Okay.' Callie agreed, leaning forward to rest her arms on the table between them. 'So, today was—'

Finn lifted an eyebrow.

'—difficult.'

Finn scratched the back of his neck. 'Difficult? No. Confusing? Hell, yeah.'

Callie broke off a piece of bread, dunked it in the oil and popped it into her mouth. Finn urged himself to be patient. She'd explain in her own time. Oh, wait—he wasn't supposed to be waiting for her explanation. *Remember the point about backing the hell up?*

'Oh, Finn, look! There's a massive bull elephant coming down to the river. Oh, he's a big boy.'

Okay, so she still wasn't ready to talk. Why did he want her to? Why did he want her to trust him with her mind, her feelings, as well as her body?

Callie leaned forward, her elbows on the table and her chin cupped in her hands. Finn couldn't resist picking up his mobile and aiming it in her direction, trying to capture the look of admiration on her face.

The flash went off, Callie blinked rapidly, and he looked down at the captured image.

Callie's eyes were scrunched closed and the image was blurry and out of focus. He deleted the image and shook his head. Well, what did he expect? It had been that type of day.

Then again, surely things could only get better from now on, he thought.

Finn leaned back in his chair and his attention was caught by a couple a short distance from them. She had a huge smile on her face and was gesticulating wildly. He just looked shocked. Fantastically happy but utterly shocked. Finn felt dread settle in his stomach. He knew what she was telling him.

The man's loud whoop and his bouncing out of his chair to lay his cheek on his partner's stomach was a pretty good clue. She was pregnant and he was excited. Finn swallowed when the guy kissed that still flat feminine stomach and then reached up to cover her mouth with his.

He understood that wave of love. He'd never loved Liz as much as he had when she'd told him he was going to be a father. He'd thought that she'd hung the moon and stars.

Unable to watch them any more, Finn turned his head and stared out onto the river, fighting the urge to tell them not to get too excited, that bad things could and did happen. Happiness could be fleeting.

Caught up in the business of the last week—the elephant rides and the game drives, the amazing sex—he'd managed to shove his grief aside. To forget, just for a little while, why he was here...with Callie. He'd managed to have a break from mourning the loss of his baby, the loss of his dream of having a family, his stepdad—all of it.

Grief, hard and sour, rolled over him and memories flashed on the big screen in his head. He saw his bedroom, the blood, Liz's white face.

He couldn't resist looking across the room again at the excited couple. He didn't know if he could ever be that excited again, ever trust in happiness like that again. Nothing compared to the joy he had felt about becoming a father, and to have it ripped away was an experience he never wanted to repeat.

Maybe in a couple of years, after a great deal of thought, he might be ready to think about another relationship, about trying to create a family with someone again, but not yet—not when he was so raw and his emotions were all over the place.

The waiter put the menu down in front of them and Finn

felt his stomach roil at the thought of food. He couldn't eat—not now. Right now he needed to be alone, to lose himself in his writing, maybe do a couple of chapters of the anecdotal travel guide he was busy compiling.

It was either that or lose himself in Callie's body. And he couldn't do that—not since he'd taken the moral high ground earlier in the day. Besides, maybe they needed a break from each other...from sex. God, did he *really* think that? Shoot him now! But he needed to step away from the quicksand and he couldn't use her as a crutch. She wouldn't be around in a couple of weeks and what would he do then? No, he had to backtrack, put some distance between them.

He was going to act like an adult now, not scuttle from the room because a random couple were expecting a baby. That was just stupidly ridiculous. He was going to sit here, enjoy the evening, the balmy night. He was with a gorgeous, entrancing woman who fascinated and frustrated him in equal measure. He was not going to fall into the vortex of grief—not tonight.

'Are you okay?' Callie asked, her eyes flashing concern.

'Sure.'

'You're not still mad at me because I acted like a looney tune today?'

'I was never mad at you.' Finn saw that she didn't buy that statement and he smiled. 'Okay, I was a little frustrated.'

'You had a right to be,' Callie admitted. She blew out a long sigh. 'I can be a very frustrating woman.'

He smiled at her self-deprecation. 'You're also a smart-ass and a flirt and as sexy as hell.'

The light dimmed in Callie's eyes. 'Yet you turned me down today?'

Finn covered her hand with his, linking their fingers. 'That wasn't because I didn't want you.'

Callie pushed her hair back with her hand. 'I know; I

was using sex as a distraction and that wasn't fair—to you or to me. I'm so sorry, Finn, it was wrong of me.'

He wanted to tell her that not five minutes ago he'd wanted to do the same thing to her, so he wasn't exactly a saint. He slid a glance to the expecting couple and sighed. God, he and Callie were a pair. Outwardly successful, talented, in the prime of their lives.

The truth was that they were both pretty screwed up in different ways.

Callie sent him a small smile. 'You keep shifting in that chair—it looks like you're uncomfortable. Why don't you move to this chair?'

Finn looked at the chair to her right and realised that it would put his back to the couple—just what he needed.

Shifting over, he settled his long length in the new chair and immediately felt more relaxed, a lot more comfortable.

Callie pushed her hand under his and slid her fingers between his. 'We're really bad talkers, aren't we? I'd rather literally spill my guts than do it emotionally, and I suspect you are the same.'

'Yeah.'

'That being said—and I know that I have absolutely no right to say this—I want you to know that if you want to talk I'll listen.'

Finn squeezed her hand, shocked at the thought that he was tempted to do just that. But they'd made a decision not to be sucked into anything deep, anything important—not to be seduced by the romance and the company and luxury.

No, he needed to put distance between them, and talking wouldn't help with that. It would just make him ache for more.

Finn squeezed her hand again. 'Back at you, angel.'

There he went again with the endearments. God, could he get *nothing* right tonight?

CHAPTER NINE

CALLIE, DRESSED IN a short terry robe, her hair wet from the shower, was curled up in the corner of a cane couch on their private veranda, a bowl of fruit salad in her hand. Finn was half perched on the railing, the riverbank vegetation below him and the mighty Zambezi river behind him, the early-morning sun beating down on his bare chest.

After their meal last night they'd both retreated to their respective corners by silent agreement. He'd gone out onto the balcony and hunched over his computer and she hadn't disturbed him. Instead she'd showered and gone to bed, taking a little time to catch up with her e-reader. She'd fallen asleep somewhere around midnight and hadn't heard Finn coming to bed, but she'd woken up curled up half on him. It had been an easy slide completely on to him and she'd sighed when he'd entered her, filling her.

It had been easy and languorous and sexy.

'Croc on the sandbank,' Finn told her, pointing so that she knew where to look.

Now or never, Hollis, Callie thought. *Are you going to back away and pretend that you didn't notice what you noticed last night? Leave the status quo? Or are you going to make this situation more complicated than it needs to be? And if you get him to open up, then he has a right to do the same to you. You ready for that? Getting to know him better will make it so much harder to walk away...*

Callie spooned up a strawberry and slowly chewed. She understood that she was taking a risk, but she knew that Finn needed someone to talk to about the horror of the last few weeks. Because it was eating him up.

When he thought she wasn't paying attention his eyes would reveal his sadness, his grief. His lower lip would tremble before he flattened it out and then he'd pull in a deep breath. Yeah, the man was in pain and he needed to talk. It was more important that he do that than it was for her to protect her heart.

Her wounds were old and mostly healed, but his were raw.

'Did you love your fiancée?'

Finn's laugh had absolutely no humour in it. 'You go straight for the jugular, don't you? I loved her, but probably not as much as I should have.'

Thought so. So, now are you going to ask the really hard question?

Yeah, she was.

'So, how far along was Liz when she miscarried?'

Finn wobbled and grabbed the railing to steady himself as the colour ran from his face. He stared at his bare feet for so long that Callie didn't think he'd ever answer her.

'Four and a half months,' Finn said finally, his voice rough. 'How did you know?'

Callie placed her bowl on the coffee table and wrapped her arms around her bent knees. 'I've always thought that there was something more to your break-up than—well, just a break-up. Then I saw your reaction to that couple last night. It was written all over your face.'

Finn grimaced. 'And I thought I hid my reaction so well.'

Callie pushed her unbrushed curls out of her eyes. 'Not so much. I take it that you really wanted the baby?'

Finn slowly nodded. 'I really did… I've always wanted to have a family—a wife, a couple of kids.'

'Because of your own dad?'

Finn took a long time to answer her. 'My dad was useless. That's the kindest word I can find to describe him. He'd come back, make these elaborate promises to us, siphon money off my mum and disappear again. It was always just Mum and I, and life was tough sometimes. I wanted a dad I could rely on.'

'James was that person for you?'

Finn nodded. 'He really was. He taught me about family.'

'And when Liz told you she was pregnant it was your chance to have the family you'd always craved?' Callie gently pushed. 'Tell me about losing your baby, Finn.'

Finn rubbed his jaw in agitation. 'She just started to bleed that night. We were at home. I've seen war—reported on war—seen some pretty horrendous stuff, but there was always a distance been me and the event. This was up close and personal. Blood…so much of it.'

That's why he got rid of the mattress, Callie realised. *Oh, Finn, honey.*

Callie knew that if she spoke, if she uttered a word of sympathy, she'd lose him.

'They took her to Theatre, did a D&C, what is that, anyway?'

'Basically, they just go in and…' Callie bit her lip '…clean everything out.'

Finn briefly closed his eyes. 'Anyway, when she came out of Theatre we had a discussion and she suggested that we break it off. She said that we were only together for the baby. That if she hadn't fallen pregnant then she doubted we would've been together any more.'

Callie's respect for Liz rose and she placed her hand on her heart. 'That was enormously brave.'

Finn frowned at her. 'What?'

Callie lifted her shoulder. 'She was brave, Finn. It would've been so much easier to go through with the wedding, to go home and pretend that you still loved each other, that you could love each other again like you should. Instead she chose the hard route—the one that took courage. Cancelling the wedding, exposing herself to gossip, to questions. In her most painful moment she looked for the truth—you've got to respect that.'

Finn stared at her. 'I never thought about it like that.'

'She deserves some credit for making a tough choice when she could've lied to herself *and* to you.' Callie smiled softly. 'You have great taste in women, Banning,' she teased.

The corner of his mouth lifted. 'Apparently so.'

'Could they tell whether your baby was a boy or a girl?'

Finn's broad shoulders rose and fell. 'I have no idea. To me it just felt right that he was a boy.'

Callie rested her chin on her kneecap. 'I bet you named him after your stepdad.'

Finn's mouth lifted at the corners in another reluctant smile. 'Witch. Yeah, I did. In my head I called him James—Jamie—same as my stepdad.'

You're still in mourning, honey, for both your stepdad and your lost little boy.

'Does anyone know, apart from me, about the baby? About what you lost?'

Finn shook his head. 'We hadn't told anyone that she was pregnant and Liz asked me to keep it like that. She's pretty private and her folks are conservative.'

'I think coping with all the questions about why you broke up so close to the wedding would be hard enough; having to explain about the miscarriage too would probably have sent her running into the night,' Callie said, empathising.

'You seem to understand her a lot better than I ever did,' Finn said, his voice sad.

'I'm a woman—and you feel bad because you wish you could've loved her more.'

Finn stared at the wild African bush that edged the opposite bank of the river and Callie sensed that it was time to be quiet, to leave him to his thoughts.

After a couple of minutes he spoke again. 'I feel stupid for mourning like this. God, I can't even call him a baby—he didn't get that far. He was an entity that I never met! That's what I've been battling with—the idea that I can be so devastated when I hadn't even met him yet.'

'Don't feel stupid. You *are* allowed to mourn losing him, Finn. It doesn't matter that his time with you was brief, or that he wasn't even fully formed yet. He was a soul and you loved him. If you lose love you are always entitled to mourn.'

'When my stepdad died—God, it was six months ago, but it still feels like it was yesterday—I lost my mentor, my rock, my best bud. Losing the baby made me feel like I'd lost him all over again.'

He might be slow to talk but, *dang*, he definitely needed to, Callie thought. This was heavy baggage to carry on your own.

Finn turned his back to her and gripped the railing with his hands, his head dropping to his chest. Callie knew that he was fighting tears and that he'd hate for her to see them.

Staying where she was, she asked another soft question. 'Did you bury your stepdad? Does he have a grave? A headstone?'

'No. He wanted his ashes scattered out at sea. Why?' Finn, now back in control, turned to face her but kept his white-knuckled grip on the railing behind him.

Callie shrugged. 'It's nice to have a place to go to remember, to cry if you need to. A place where you can think about your stepfather and your son.'

'It's a nice idea, but I don't.' Finn released the railing and walked over to the coffee table. He drained the half-glass of orange juice he'd left there earlier. 'Can we change the subject? I'm feeling a bit like a specimen under a microscope.'

Callie looked up at him and saw his shuttered eyes, his now implacable face. Yeah, he was done talking. And that was okay, she thought. She'd got a lot more out of him than she'd expected to.

And she'd given him something in return. She wasn't sure what. Maybe a little comfort, a little support. And that was more than okay—she had it and he needed it.

She was beginning to think that there wasn't much that she *wouldn't* give Finn.

Including, if she wasn't very, very careful, her heart.

After Livingstone they were sent back to South Africa and booked into a sprawling, Vegas-type casino on the outskirts of the country's capital. Callie had been looking forward to this portion of their trip the most, but instead of loving it, as she'd expected to do, she wanted to go back to easy summer days and hot summer nights—in bed as well as out.

She didn't want fancy rooms or air-conditioning. She wanted to hear the call of the fish eagles, to smell the electricity of a wild storm. She didn't want to hear the *ker-ching* of slot machines or the whoops of overdressed, over-perfumed people.

Callie leaned back in her chair in the restaurant section of a popular bar and hoped Finn wouldn't take his time fetching her wrap from their hotel room. Then again, their room was about a mile from the entertainment area, so she might only see him again in an hour or two.

Callie gave a man approaching her table a look that said *don't even think about trying to chat me up* and he halted in his tracks and turned away. Fishing her mobile out of her purse, she pushed a speed dial number and blocked her other ear so that she could hear when Rowan answered.

'Uh…Cal. I didn't expect you to call tonight.'

'Why?' Callie demanded, laughter in her voice. 'Are you out having fun with my wicked witch of a mother?'

The long silence that followed her comment was all the confirmation she needed. Callie felt her stomach cramp and she stared at the table, fighting the burning sensation in her eyes.

'Where are you?' she croaked out.

'Awelfor,' Rowan finally answered.

'He allowed her to come *home*?'

'Callie—'

Callie heard a familiar guffaw in the background and her clenching stomach launched up her throat. 'Is my dad there?'

'Yeah, Seb invited him and Annie round for dinner.'

'With *Laura*?' Callie clasped her neck with her hand. 'Am I the only one who still has a problem with the fact that she left for over twenty years and we haven't heard from her since? That she abandoned me—us? How can you all just sit there and laugh and drink and pretend what she did was okay?'

'Honey—'

'Don't *honey* me. God, you all suck…' Callie whispered into the phone, before jamming her finger against the red button.

Hauling in air, she looked around for a waiter but there wasn't one to be seen. She needed a drink and she needed it now. More than that, she needed to forget that her family—the people who were supposed to love her most—were laughing and drinking and eating with Laura as if she'd done no wrong. How could they just forget? Just forgive?

And her dad? How *could* he? He was supposed to be on her side.

She didn't want to think about her mother and she couldn't consider forgetting or forgiving. No, what she needed was a distraction. Something to take her mind off her mother, her family and the aching void in her heart.

Callie looked around and through the window to a pub, where she saw a group of well-dressed adults. They looked sophisticated and successful and badly in need of a party.

Well, *she* was their girl.

He'd lost his fake wife, Finn thought, bemused, holding her wrap in his hand and back in the restaurant where he'd left her. Finding Callie was going to be a nightmare. Was it asking too much for her to have stayed where he'd left her?

Hearing a loud chorus of male laughter from the adjacent pub, Finn had a sinking feeling that he'd find her wherever the action was—and it sounded as if the action was next door.

Heading that way, he walked through the frosted doors and there she was, standing behind the bar, a bottle of tequila in her hand, happily pouring shots into the grubby glasses lined up in front of her. The bartender next to her had two bottles in his hand and was filling up the glasses too.

A mound of lemon segments sat on the plate in front of the fifteen-strong crowd and Finn shook his head when he saw that there were women in the group as well. It seemed that Callie could charm members of her own sex into drinking competitions as well.

He'd only been gone an hour. How the hell had she get managed to get front and centre and drinking in sixty minutes? God, bartenders must love her. Finn shook his head as Callie licked salt off her hand, tossed back her drink and sucked on her lemon, pulling the inevitable 'tequila face'.

She was a handful, and a man would have to have steel balls to take her on.

You are not that man, he reminded himself. *You are not in a place where you can even think about getting emotionally involved with another woman; Callie is your rebound fling. It doesn't matter that she totally gets you about the miscarriage, that she understands how it feels to lose something you've never had, that she's fun and smart and so sexy.*

It was the wrong time and place. He'd thought long and hard about getting involved with Liz, longer and harder about Liz moving into his house, and here he was, after a few short weeks, thinking about taking on a girl with a wild streak.

It would be crazy. And yet a reckless part of him wanted to. He wondered what it would be like to love her, to be loved by her. To have her there when he came home, to think about her when he was away. And he knew that he *would* think about her when he was gone—he knew that he wouldn't be able to compartmentalise her as easily as he had Liz.

Callie would demand so much more from him than Liz—or any other woman he'd ever met.

He didn't have it in him—not now and not any time soon—to give her a quarter of what she wanted or expected. Or deserved. Callie deserved the world and he didn't have it in him to give it to her.

'Hey, hubby!' Callie waved the tequila bottle at him, her eyes slightly squinty.

Finn pushed through the crowd to stand directly opposite her. 'You're on the wrong side of the bar, wife. How did you get there?'

Callie smiled broadly and pointed to a sophisticated-looking couple. 'Kelvin and Neil are celebrating their anniversary and these are all their friends!'

'Uh-huh?'

'And I offered to buy them a drink—to toast them—and they said yes, and then we got talking about our favourite shooters, and I showed Grant here—' she laid a hand on the barmen's shoulder '—how to make a champagne shooter, and we had some of those. Now we're doing it old school.'

'Ah...' Finn winced at the thought of what she'd spent, throwing liquor down strangers' throats. Correction: what *he* was about to spend—because Callie, dressed in a slinky black cocktail dress, certainly didn't have a credit card tucked between her magnificent breasts or under the thin cord of her tiny, tiny thong. He knew this because—well, because he'd happily watched her climb into, and out of, and back into that dress hours earlier.

And he couldn't put the booze on his hotel bill—even *he* wouldn't get away with forty-plus shooters on his expense account.

One half of the anniversary couple stood up and held his hand out for Finn to shake. He looked more sober than the rest of his crew. 'Your wife is an absolute delight and such a hoot.'

'Thank you,' Finn replied, looking at his wife, who was leaning across the bar, squishing her boobs with her elbows and giving herself a hell of a cleavage. Even the gay boys seemed fascinated by the view. Her breasts might be spectacular, but he was distracted by the fact that her eyes were more violet than blue—a colour he'd come to associate with Callie being upset or sad.

'Something happen while I was gone, angel?' he asked quietly.

Her smile was bright and bold and perfectly suited to this fake place. 'Yeah, I started a party! I haven't done that for a while. I have my mojo back!'

Oh, yeah, something had happened. Another call from her mother? Maybe…

'Honey, you never lost it.' He jerked his head as he put his hand in his back pocket to pull out his wallet. 'Time to go, angel.' He flipped open his wallet and pulled out a credit card, which he handed to the amused barman.

'Awww, I don't wanna…' Callie whined.

'I have a surprise for you waiting in our room,' Finn lied.

He just had to get her to the room; he knew that as soon as Callie fell onto the bed she'd be dead to the world, and he doubted that she'd remember that he promised her a surprise. After all, tequila was well known for its coma-inducing and amnesiac qualities.

As he'd suspected Callie's eyes lit up, and she skipped around Grant to come over to his side of the bar. 'What is it?'

'You'll have to wait and see.' Finn took the credit card slip and his eyes widened at the total. Damn! How many shooters and how many bottles of champagne had they gone through?

The barman sent him a sympathetic look. 'Sorry, sir.'

'She's going to bankrupt me,' Finn muttered, taking back his card. 'Let's go before you do any more damage.'

'Got to say goodbye first,' Callie told him, and Finn waited while she kissed cheeks and exchanged hugs as if she was saying goodbye to her best friends. Good grief, she'd only met these people an hour or so ago.

'Be happy, people!' Callie yelled at them as he steered her towards the door.

Most of them—Callie included—were certainly not going to be happy in the morning.

Callie rolled over in the massive bed and feeling as if she had a bowling ball bouncing off the inside of her skull.

There was a time, she thought on an internal whimper, when she could party herself stupid and wake up the next morning raring to go.

That time had passed, she decided mournfully. Squinting, she sat up on her elbows and forced her eyes open to look at the gold and white garish suite. *Ack.* If her husband—real, that was—had brought her here for her honeymoon she'd have stabbed him between the eyes with a fork.

Talking about husbands—where was hers?

He'd slept with her—she had a recollection of him waking her up to swallow some aspirin some time close to dawn—but she didn't recall him leaving their bed. She needed him right now. Mostly to order coffee and to hand her some more aspirin.

Note to self: *I can no longer drink like a twenty-year-old.*

Second note to self: *tequila is nasty and no longer your friend.*

But her brother and her best friend and her father and soon-to-be stepmother had spent last night laughing and drinking and socialising with Laura.

She'd wanted a distraction, to forget, and it had worked for a while. But this morning she still felt hurt and betrayed and she had a hangover. Talk about adding fuel to the fire. Callie tucked her hand under her cheek, ignoring the trickle of tears leaking from her eyes.

Hurting, she wondered if she was being harsh in not wanting to engage with Laura. *Was* she just being stubborn? Unfair? Why was reconnecting with her so much easier for Seb than it was for her?

She closed her eyes and remembered those long nights sobbing in her room, her ten, fifteen, eighteen-year-old self wondering what had been so wrong with Laura's life— with *her*—that she'd had to leave. What had she and her dad and Seb done that was so wrong that she'd had to leave and never call or write? Was she sick…poor—dead?

She'd spent most of her nights worrying about Laura and her days pretending that she was fine, so that her father and Seb wouldn't worry about her.

It had taken all the emotional energy she had.

And now she was supposed to just wipe her past away because Laura had decided that it was time to reconnect? *No*.

Callie felt the bed dip behind her and Finn's warm, broad hand stroking her bare back. Within seconds she felt comforted, calmer, as if she could cope with whatever life threw at her. What was it about this man that made her feel both brave and safe at the same time?

Finn was on her side, totally in her corner, all hers. Just as she'd known he would be.

'Angel, why the tears?'

She couldn't not tell him. It was her turn to let him in.

Callie rolled over and rested her forearm over her eyes. 'Something happened last night.'

'I know. What did your mother do?'

He just *got it*, she thought on an internal sigh. He got *her*. 'Had dinner with my father and brother and my best friend in my childhood home.'

'And you're mad at her? And them?' Finn pulled her arm from her eyes before rubbing a thumb over her cheekbone. 'I brought you aspirin and coffee; take them and we'll talk.'

Callie groaned as she pulled herself up so that she was leaning back against the padded headboard, the sheet tucked up under her arms. She picked the tablets out of Finn's hand and chased them down with a glass of water. He passed her a large mug of coffee, which she gratefully took.

Finn sat next to her, calm and strong, and his strength

seemed to flow into her. She could start to rely on having him around, she thought, having his calm presence in her life.

'So, start from the beginning and tell me about Laura.'

'It's a long story.'

'Nowhere else I need to be. No one else more important than you right now.'

She could see that truth in his eyes. Right now, right here, she was the most important person in his life and she loved it. Oh, dear God, if she wasn't careful she could love him.

Callie looked at his hand, big and tanned on her thigh. She took another sip of coffee before placing it on the bedside table. *Park any thoughts about love and for ever and talk to him,* Callie told herself. *You need to talk to someone.*

Pushing her curls behind her ears, she started trying to explain. 'I told you that I was a hell-on-wheels child. I tried anything once. And I mean anything, I had absolutely no sense of self-preservation. The highest tree, the tallest rock, the fastest bike, the biggest wave. Unfortunately I always bit off more than I could chew. The nurses and doctors at our nearest casualty department knew me by name.'

Callie drew invisible patterns on the sheet with her index finger.

'It was after another visit to Casualty, when my dad brought me home—with a broken arm and two cracked ribs—that we found out that that Laura had left us. For good.'

Finn held her thigh and his eyes encouraged her to go on. She'd never told anyone this before, but she felt safe with Finn.

'In my childish head I equated my being a wild child with her leaving. And, because I'm me, I thought, *What the hell? Let's make damn sure she had a good excuse for going.* I let it rip. I was wild, Finn. Crazy. I did stupid things, took incredible risks, put myself in danger. I went walking the streets at night, looking for trouble. I caught trains and buses into bad areas. I hitchhiked all over the place. I surfed huge waves, was a maniac on my skateboard and on my bike. Thank God that He protects the stupid.'

'Why did you do all of that?'

'Partly to justify her leaving—*Look how bad I am. I don't blame you for leaving*—and also because the adrenalin high was so damn good. I think I was also challenging my father's and brother's love. If they didn't walk away from me when I was so bad then they *did* love me. Crazy, huh?'

Finn stretched out beside her and rested his hand on her stomach. 'Not so much.'

'Anyway, the craziness got me out of my head, stopped me from feeling worthless and abandoned, and I craved it.' Callie stared at her hands. 'In my late teens that adrenalin high started to be more difficult to achieve and I started flirting with alcohol.'

She saw sympathy on his face, in his eyes, but not pity. She couldn't have handled pity.

'I got drunk and wrecked my car. I was damn lucky not to die.'

Finn swore. 'Angel...'

'Yeah. Well, that prompted my father and brother to tear me a new one and I was finally brought under control. I made a big deal of their authority and bossiness but secretly I loved it. I started to believe that they loved me and always would, and I promised them that I wouldn't do anything stupid again. So I cut out all the extreme stuff except the partying and grew up, I suppose.'

Finn looked puzzled. 'Yet that day in Livingstone you were prepared to break your promise to go bungee jumping? Oh, wait. It was a coping mechanism.'

'I needed to escape from myself. When she phoned I

didn't want to deal with all the old feelings that bubbled to the surface and I reverted to what worked. Sex with you or…' she pulled a face '…something else to make the adrenalin pump.'

Finn smiled. 'That's a hell of a backhanded compliment, Cal, but I'll take it.'

Callie couldn't smile—not just yet. 'God, it all sounds so stupid.' She pulled a face. 'It makes sense in my head.'

Finn's thumb stroked her knee. 'I'm not judging you, angel.'

Callie went on to explain how hurt she'd felt by her family having dinner with her mother and her need for distraction—which had prompted the party in the bar.

Finn took a sip of her coffee before asking, 'And you really don't want to see your mum? Meet her? Get an explanation?'

Callie shrugged. 'Do you think I should?' she asked.

His opinion was important to her; she respected and trusted it. And him. She trusted *him*. Dear God, she really did.

'I can't decide that for you, Cal. I can give you another perspective on it, but I would never presume to tell you what to do. First tell me why you're so against meeting her.'

Callie placed her hand on his and stared down at their linked hands. 'I haven't seen or heard from her in over twenty years. What's there to say? She missed out on every important day of my life and now she wants to make contact. Where was she when I needed a mother? Hotfooting it around the world! She chose to leave. I'm choosing not to acknowledge her return.' Callie lifted worried eyes to his. 'Am I wrong, Finn? Should I be able to just forgive her?'

'Again, no judging.' Finn lifted her hand and placed a kiss on her knuckles. 'Cal, my father is a shocking father and I have no freaking clue where he is. I worry about him, and sometimes I wish I could just talk to him, know that he's okay and find out why he made the choices he did. I'm not saying that I'd accept or forgive those choices— I'd just like to understand why he made them. And my two real parents are dead. I'd do anything to spend some more time with *them*.'

Finn spoke quietly but his voice was full of conviction and Callie listened carefully, soaking in his words.

'The other thing to consider is what if Laura chooses to stay in Cape Town? If she becomes part of your brother's life again? What then?'

Callie looked horrified. 'Oh, God, I never considered that possibility. I'm so close to Seb and Rowan… I would have to see her at family functions…' Callie closed her eyes. 'It would be horrible if we couldn't speak to one another. Oh, God, maybe I should just meet her.'

'Take a breath, honey. It's just something to consider. Cross one bridge at a time,' Finn told her, squeezing her hand to reassure her. 'You don't need to make any rash decisions—you just need to think it all through. You need to try and separate your emotions from your decision.'

'I don't know if I can.'

Finn kissed her bare shoulder. 'I believe in you. I believe that you can move mountains if you want to. You are one of the strongest women I have ever met.' He smiled into her skin. 'Crazy as a loon, but strong as hell.'

At his words Callie fell a little deeper, a little harder. This man might be exactly what she needed.

'How is your head?'

'Better.' Callie lifted her hand to her head and nodded. 'Yeah, definitely better.' She also felt lighter, because Finn had just listened without judgement. Acceptance, Callie thought. It was such a rare and beautiful thing.

'You hungry?'

'Starving!' Callie replied.

'Room Service? Or do you want to brave the hordes downstairs?' Finn asked.

Callie winced. 'Room Service, please.'

Finn nodded, his dimple flashing. He leaned back, his hands spread out on the covers, and cocked his head at her. 'So…how hungry are you really? Can breakfast wait?'

Callie tipped her head at his playful expression. 'Why?'

'I just thought that maybe you needed a rush of adrenalin? Please say yes.'

Callie's smile made her eyes crinkle and she placed a hand over them. 'Oh, God, I'm *so* going to regret telling you that.'

Finn placed his hands on her shoulders and pushed her onto her back. 'That wasn't a no. I didn't hear a no, so I'm going to take that as a yes.'

Callie sighed theatrically as she linked her hands around his neck and pulled his mouth down to hers. 'If you must…'

CHAPTER TEN

BUSH AND BEACH, Callie thought, digging her toes into the white sands of the Mozambique coastline. This was, hands-down, the best holiday of her life. And five days at the exceptionally luxurious, remote Manta Ray Lodge, on the Bazaruto Archipelago, was the best way to end their trip.

Callie sat up on her elbows and watched Finn walk out of the gentle surf, heading towards her after snorkelling above the reef just behind the breakers. He loved the sea, she realised. From scuba-diving to deep-sea fishing, to snorkelling, to kite-surfing—he wanted to do it all. She could easily see why he was so good at his job as a travel writer. He threw himself into every experience he was offered, wringing every drop of pleasure he could from the situation.

He was so gorgeous, she thought, watching as he walked up the beach to where she was lying on a towel in the sand. Tall, ripped, in peak physical condition. Hair pushed off his face and red board shorts clinging to those strong thighs. So drool-worthy.

She knew that body intimately—knew every toned muscle, every scar, the fact that one of his little toes was crooked. She knew that scraping her nails across his abs made him shiver and that he hated her blowing in his ear. She knew that he didn't have a favourite sexual position, that he liked to mix it up, and that he loved oral sex. That he could kiss her for hours without taking it further, that he always slept on his stomach, and that he needed to run or do a workout and have at least two cups of coffee in the morning before he could string a sentence together.

She knew he was loyal and responsible and that he loved his stepbrothers, and that he was mentally and physically tough. She also knew that she was on the very slippery slope to falling in love—if she wasn't there already. He was what she hadn't known she was looking for.

And he didn't want her—not like that. It wasn't part of the arrangement...the deal. *No hearts and flowers,* she'd said. How often had she said that? Along with *Don't let me be seduced, This is short-term, This is going to end.*

Use, abuse and toss.

She'd broken every rule they'd laid out from the beginning. She'd been so arrogant, thinking that she could control herself, control the situation, control her response to him. Life was rolling on the floor, laughing its ass off at her.

Even though she knew they couldn't be anything more she wanted to dream about a future with him. But there wasn't one—couldn't be one. Their jobs kept them both buzzing around the world, and she didn't need a man complicating her life—especially now. She had a mother who, after being absent for most of her life, was doing a very good job of that all by herself.

Was she just being seduced by the holiday? The romance of their surroundings? This wasn't real life. Real life had bills and work and family and jobs to complicate the situation. There was a reason holiday romances never worked out.

There wasn't any future for them. *Was there?*

Callie lifted her head as Finn approached her and sighed when his lips brushed hers in a gesture that felt so natural, so right. *Holiday romance,* she reminded herself, *not going to last.*

'I saw a scorpion fish and a small manta ray.'

'Cool…' Callie murmured as he dropped onto the hot sand next to her.

Finn looked around, catching the eye of a hovering waiter who walked over to them. Finn ordered a beer and Callie ordered a bottle of water.

'This is the life,' Finn stated, reaching for his sunglasses, which he'd left on top of her beach bag. He slipped them on and leaned back on his elbows, stretching like a cat in the sun.

Those sleek muscles rippled under tanned skin and Callie couldn't believe that her libido was buzzing again. She swallowed the urge to suggest they head back to their private, practically-in-the-sea chalet, just fifty metres away from them, so that she could worship that body. Instead she half turned, stretched out, and rested the back of her head on Finn's thigh.

'Talk to me.'

Above his wraparound shades a dark eyebrow lifted. 'Okay. About what?'

Callie sat up, put her back to the sea and faced him. 'Do you ever think of Liz? Do you miss her?' she asked, eyes down, wiggling in the sand.

'We were together for five years, Cal…so, yeah. I do.' Finn replied, his voice low. 'I was supposed to be sharing all this with her.'

Damn, that was a knife to her heart. 'I know. I'm sorry.'

'I'm not.'

Callie's head shot up and she met his rueful eyes. 'I don't understand.'

'She was right to call it quits. We'd stopped loving each other. Our marriage would never have lasted.' Finn pushed his hand through his hair, his eyes still on the sea. 'Getting married seemed like a good idea at the time. We'd talked about it and we'd been together for a long time. When she fell pregnant it seemed like the next step to take—a natural progression,' Finn explained. 'Then she lost the baby, and our last reason to be together was removed.'

'Do you see yourself in a relationship again?'

Finn took a long time to answer. 'I think I need to be on my own for a while.'

No surprised there, Callie thought.

'I never jump into situations with my eyes closed, Callie. I think everything through. I don't do quick and impulsive and crazy. Relationships that are meant to last take time and are hard work.'

His words rumbled over her and she could hear the conviction in his tone.

'I'm pretty sure that I don't want a long-distance relationship again, but that's all I can have until I give up my job and find something else to do. And that's not going to happen any time soon.'

You, me, us—we're not going to happen either. Callie heard his unspoken words. *That wasn't the deal.*

Callie stretched out her legs and dug her toes into the sand, her eyes burning behind her dark glasses. 'I'm really glad that I was able to be your rebound girl, Finn.'

Finn linked her hand in his. 'Maybe you should try being in a relationship some time, Cal.'

She forced herself to sound jovial, carefree. 'How come you get to be footloose and fancy-free but I should settle down?' she asked, making sure that she had a small smile on her face.

'Because you've only *ever* been footloose and fancy-free. I think that you would be a brilliant partner: you're fun, intelligent, and crazy good in the sack.'

Finn pushed his sunglasses into his hair and she caught her breath at the passion and...*affection?*...she saw in his eyes.

'And you'd be a stunning mum one day.'

Callie instinctively shook her head. 'Yeah, *that's* not going to happen.'

'Why not?' Finn asked gently.

Callie folded her arms against her chest and shook her head. 'I'm never putting any child through what my mother did to me!'

Finn grabbed her chin and tipped her head up, making her meet his eyes. 'Honey, you would never do to your kid what your mum did to you. No way, no how.'

Callie swallowed the lump in her throat. 'How do you know? I'm selfish, I bounce around the world, I'm totally self-involved.'

'No, you're not. That's who you pretend to be.' Finn cupped the side of her face in his broad palm. 'When you decide that you're strong enough to be brave, when you find someone you love enough to risk your heart, you'll hand it over because you're so damn generous. And when you bring a kid into the world you'll be incredible at that— because you know how not having a mum affected *you*.'

'I don't know if I can do either—hand my heart over *or* have a kid,' Callie admitted.

'One day...' Finn said, lying back in the sand and placing a forearm over his eyes. 'I can almost guarantee it.'

Except that right now, holiday romance or not, Callie thought bitterly, *I can't imagine doing that with anyone else but you.*

Stupid girl, she thought, standing up and walking to the super-clear water. She waded in, waiting for it to become deep enough so that she could dive. *That's why you shouldn't have deep conversations with Finn...why you should keep it light and frothy.*

Because deep conversations raised possibilities that she wasn't ready to think about or deal with. Deep conversations gave birth to dreams that would never come true, possibilities that would never be realised.

Wishes that would never be fulfilled.

After a light lunch of freshly caught prawns and garden salad, accompanied by a glass of dry white wine, Finn and Callie headed back to their room to escape the intensity of the midday sun. The private villa, tucked away into the palm trees just off the beach, was incredibly private—perfect for a honeymoon couple.

Except they weren't on honeymoon, Finn reminded himself again. She was his fake wife and they were having a very temporary affair. But for a moment just now on the beach he'd been tempted to suggest that he and Callie try and extend it into real life.

Then he'd pulled himself back to reality. Callie was a stunning travelling companion: easy to look at, fun to talk to, great in bed.

The end.

Despite sharing their secrets, the mental and physical connection they had, she'd never once hinted at wanting anything more from him, wanting to change the rules. *She* knew that this was a holiday romance, so why was he suddenly doubting it? What the hell was he thinking?

Finn closed his eyes and shook his head. Goddammit, he was losing his mind. This trip was not real life—this was an aberration, a step out of time. It wouldn't be like this every trip. It was usually hectic: a combination of stunning sights and experiences interrupted by long periods of boredom spent in hotel rooms and airport lounges.

It wasn't a life to build a relationship on. As for another long-distance one? Well, that hadn't worked out so well the last time he'd tried it, and Callie wasn't the type of girl he'd be able to stay away from for long.

Finn walked over to the small fridge in the corner of the

lounge area and took out a bottle of water. Cracking the lid, he took a long drink and watched Callie as she pulled her T-shirt up and over her head, revealing the top half of the pink and orange bikini she was wearing. A vision of her, round and bursting with life with his child, flashed across his retina and he groaned. No, he wasn't going to think of her in terms of for ever, in terms of creating a family with her.

Or being the man she fell in love with.

He wanted to be single, to get his bearings, and she was even more wary of commitment than he was. Why did he want to put his fist through that glass door at the thought of her loving and living with someone else? Handing over that very fragile heart to another man?

He was just projecting, influenced by the incredibleness of these past two weeks. This wasn't reality.

Get a grip, Banning. She's fun, good company and brilliant in the sack. That's it. You have less than a week left of this—of her—so get your head out of your ass, stop obsessing, and catch a clue. Instead of standing here, staring at her like a moonstruck whipped boy, do something!

So he would do what he…they…did best. Lose themselves in each other…

He gestured with his water bottle. 'Carry on,' he told her.

Callie lifted her eyebrows at him. 'Sorry?'

Her voice was prissy, but her sexy smile told him that she knew where he wanted to go and was happy to tag along.

'Shorts off.'

Callie's eyes deepened with passion as she slowly pulled down the zip to her brief denim shorts and shimmied them over her hips. When they dropped to the floor he looked at her standing there in the shadows, the shades drawn to keep the heat out.

'Top off,' he said in a croaky voice, and took another sip of water to moisten his mouth.

Callie reached behind her back and pulled one of the ties holding her top together before reaching for the other one around her neck. The two triangles joined her shorts on the floor and she placed her fists on her hips and stared at him.

He was rock-hard and ready to spring out of his pants—and he hadn't even touched her yet. Surely after so much sex he should be able to temper his reaction to her by now? But it took just one look into those amazing eyes for him to be ready to roll. Surely he should have more control?

Then Callie stepped out of her bikini panties and he knew that, with her, he had absolutely no control at all.

As he reached for her he wondered how he was supposed to walk away from her. From the amazing sex but also, even harder, from her sharp mind, her dirty sense of humour and the vulnerable, soft soul beneath that vivacious personality?

How?

It was past eleven at night when their plane finally landed in Cape Town, and nearly midnight when Finn swung his SUV into the driveway in front of her closed-up house. This was unlike any homecoming she'd ever experienced, Callie thought, staring at her tightly laced hands in her lap. She didn't want to be here, back in the city. She didn't want to go back to real life, to work, to a life without Finn to wake up to, to make love with, to snuggle up to at night.

She wanted to be back in Kruger, in the sweltering heat of Livingstone, on that white sand beach. Anywhere with Finn...everywhere with Finn.

Finn's white-knuckled hands gripped the steering wheel. 'So, this is it.'

Callie sucked in her top lip. 'Yep.'

'How long are you in the country for?' Finn asked, his voice low.

'I think I have a quick trip scheduled to Milan for next week. You?'

'Not sure. I have to get this article in and accepted, then I can choose between a dude ranch in Montana or the northern lights in Alaska.'

Callie made herself pat his shoulder. 'Poor guy. I'm sure both will be terrible,' she teased, and felt proud of herself. She wouldn't make this goodbye difficult by weeping and wailing. She would hold her head up high and go out on a huge smile.

Finn turned his head to look at her. 'They won't be as much fun without you.'

Callie felt the tears well. 'You can't say that. I'm trying to be brave, here,' she protested.

'Me too.' Finn blew out a long sigh before dropping his head back onto the headrest. He rolled his head to look at her. His eyes, deep with regret, caught and held hers. 'I still want you.'

Callie swallowed and her hand instinctively reached out to grip his thigh. 'I know. I want you too.'

'Last time for the road?'

'It's a really bad idea, Finn.'

'I know, but let's do it anyway. I need to burn you into my memory one last time.'

The next morning, for the first time in weeks, Callie didn't wake up to Finn laying hot, wet kisses down her back, or a hard, heavy arm across her waist, or warm male breath tickling her ear.

She was alone and she really didn't like it.

Rolling over, she looked at the dent his head had left on the pillow and, inexplicably, felt tears burn her eyes. How was she supposed to live without him? Be without him?

Exist without him? How was she supposed to love him if he wasn't even around?

Love? Was she in love? Could she be?

This was insane. Nobody fell in love after a month—especially her, a girl who didn't believe in love and happily-ever-after. But she couldn't deny it any more. She loved Finn—absolutely, utterly, probably catastrophically.

Callie sat up in bed and rested her head on her bent knees. This was *so* not a clever thing to have done. Finn was on the rebound—he didn't want a relationship, wasn't interested. She knew all this, but *she* was.

Should she tell him? A part of her wanted to, needed to. Callie had loved too few people in her life, had been loved by too few, to bury or ignore this amazing sensation when it came her way. It was what it was and it demanded to be expressed—to be validated, to be acknowledged. But she'd also told him that there would be no hearts and flowers, no demands for anything more, no complications. Was telling him that she loved him more important than keeping her promise? Especially since she knew that he didn't feel the same way about her?

What should she do?

Callie lifted her head when she heard footsteps outside her door and made herself look at him as he stepped into her bedroom. She had to look at him because she didn't know when she would again.

If she would again...

Love was love, but that didn't automatically translate into happily-ever-after. She knew that now. Her mother had said she loved her but she hadn't stayed; she loved Finn, and even if by some miracle he felt the same they had so many obstacles in their way. They both travelled extensively. How could they mesh their schedules so that they could build a relationship? Maintain it?

But she was getting way ahead of herself. She still had to decide whether to tell him or not.

'Hey, you're awake,' Finn said, handing her a cup of coffee.

'I am. Thanks.' Callie took the coffee and took a grateful sip, thankful for a reason not to talk.

'I brought your bags in,' Finn said, moving to look out of her window to the view of the sea.

Callie cocked her head at his quiet voice and knew that he was trying to ease his way out of her bedroom and her life. His fists were bunched in his pockets and his lips were pulled tight.

'I checked my email while you were sleeping. I'm heading for Alaska.'

Callie felt as if the coffee was threatening to come up her throat again. 'When?' she asked, her throat hoarse.

'Within a day or two.'

'That soon, huh?'

Callie carefully placed her coffee cup on the side table and swung her legs out of bed. Reaching for a robe that hung over the back of her chair, she pulled it on. Her hands were shaky as she tied it at the waist.

'So this is definitely goodbye?'

Finn turned and sat on the open windowsill. 'It should have been goodbye last night. We just make it harder the longer we draw this out.' His voice was low, but resolute.

He had no idea how hard it could be, Callie thought. He wasn't in love with her but she was with him.

'Do you think you'll ever fall in love again?' she asked, as a way to test these very turbulent waters. Just to make sure...

Finn's head snapped up in surprise at the question. 'I'm not sure I was in the first place.' He raked a hand through his hair. 'I don't know... I don't think so. If I was so inclined then it would've been with you, during this last month.'

Callie struggled to keep him from seeing how those words pierced her soul. She used every acting skill she had to make her voice sound light and flirty.

'So you're not in love with me, then?' she asked him, deliberately batting her eyelashes.

'Nope. Why? Are you in love with me?' Finn teased back, and she was faced with the do or die question.

Did she admit it and have their relationship end on an awkward, weird note—or did she let him leave her life thinking she was unaffected?

Never had a choice been so hard.

She tipped her head and dredged up a big, bold smile. 'What would you say if I told you I was?'

Finn took his time answering. 'I'd tell you what I've been telling myself: that we're blinded by the passion between us, that we stepped out of the reality of daily life and the romantic settings and the warm weather and the luxury changed the way we behaved. That we can't trust out judgement.'

Callie nodded. She'd thought about all of that, but none of it had changed her mind or her knowledge of what *was*. She loved him. Simply. Crazily. For ever.

He didn't love her. Oh, she knew that he loved her body, loved sex with her, but it wasn't the same thing. Callie rubbed her forehead with her fingers as her mind operated at warp speed, trying to decide what to do.

Then Finn took the decision out of her hands by walking over to her and kissing her gently on the lips before folding her into his strong arms.

'We agreed to walk away, Cal.'

Callie looked up at him, feeling so safe in the circle of his arms. Arms that would soon be gone. 'Guess it's time to rip off those rose-coloured glasses and get back to real life, huh?'

'In a couple of days…weeks…we'll settle down into that real life and this will feel like a dream.'

Callie buried her face in his neck. 'So I'll always be your dream girl?'

'You bet.' Finn stroked her hair. His long sigh blew into her curls. 'This wasn't supposed to get this tangled, this complicated.'

Still no *I love you*.

Callie tried to swallow the golf ball that was lodged in her throat. 'I'll miss you. Thanks for a brilliant time.'

'I'll miss you too. Thanks for being a brilliant fake wife.' Finn kissed the top of her head—the brush-off kiss for any man—and stepped away from her. 'Take care, Callie. And think about what I said about your mother.'

'Yeah.'

In her eagerness to avoid the first person who'd broken her heart she'd run away with a second person who'd just rebroken it. She had the intelligence of a pot plant, Callie thought, watching him walk across her lounge to the front door.

'Bye, angel.'

It took every iota of willpower she had, and then some, not to throw her arms around his knees and beg him not to go.

'Bye.'

Then the door snicked closed behind him and she felt her heart cleave in two. Overwhelmed, she sank to the floor and wrapped her arms around her head, trying to shield herself from the burning miasma of pain that engulfed her.

It didn't help, she realised. Nothing would—not for a while. She knew this. She'd been here before.

CHAPTER ELEVEN

CALLIE MADE HERSELF get up the next morning, forced herself to put on a pretty dress, curl her hair and do her makeup. Her world might be falling apart but there was no reason for people to know that she was too. Besides, if she pretended hard enough and long enough that everything was fine then maybe it would be. Eventually.

She was making herself a smoothie, in an effort to start losing the pounds she'd picked up drinking cocktails on the beach with he-whose-name-could-not-be-mentioned, when her doorbell rang. She considered ignoring it and had just decided to do that when it pealed again.

Dammit! Thinking that she wasn't in the mood to see anyone, to explain anything, she stomped through to the front door and looked through the peephole at the distorted image of a tall blonde woman. It took her a minute to recognise the blue, blue eyes of Laura, the tall frame, the long face.

She looked older, Callie thought, her heart accelerating. An older, harder, tougher *me*. Even through the peephole she could see that she looked as if she'd lived a hard life—too much sun, booze, too many cigarettes. Callie wanted to tell her to go away, that she didn't want to see her, but she couldn't push any words past her thick tongue.

'Cal-belle? Honey?'

Callie could hear her voice clearly through the wooden door.

'I know that you're there. I heard your footsteps.'

Cal-Belle. God, she hadn't heard that in over twenty years. Her mum's pet name for her—Laura's pet name for her.

'Callie, I know that you don't want to see me, and I understand why. I do—I really do. But I just couldn't leave, fly back to Sao Paulo, without trying at least once.'

Callie kept silent but let Laura speak. She wanted to be strong enough to walk away but she couldn't—not yet.

'There's so much I want to say to you, so much I want to explain.'

Callie, feeling drained and very, very vulnerable, didn't even realise that hot, thick tears were rolling down her face. All she could think was that she wanted Finn... needed Finn. She needed his strong arms to hold her up, his voice in her ear telling her that she was okay, that she would always be okay, that she could do this.

But he wasn't here. Like her mother, when she needed him most he was AWOL. The people she loved most had the ability to let her down the hardest.

Hardening her heart, she finally managed to speak. 'I'm not ready to talk to you, Laura. I don't know if I'll ever be ready.'

She didn't think she could even open the door.

'I've made a lot of mistakes, Callie, but the biggest one was walking out on you and your brother.'

You think?

'I want to tell you that I'm sorry, and if this is the only way I get to do it—through a closed door—then this is how I'll do it.'

Callie slipped off her shoes and quickly moved to the right, to the thin sliver of tinted glass that allowed her to see out but kept visitors from looking in. Laura was looking at her fingernails and her foot was tapping on the terracotta tiles. She looked bone-deep scared.

Callie remembered what she'd said to Finn about Liz, about how courageous her decision to end their relationship had been. Wasn't it equally courageous of Laura to face her, to ask for forgiveness after so long? She had to know that it wouldn't be easy, that she might not get it, but she was still willing to try.

Her mother was standing there offering an explanation—something that Finn desperately wanted from his own father. And she was alive. Finn's parents weren't. If she turned Laura away now, would she regret it for the rest of her life?

'Callie?'

'Can you hang on a sec? I just need a moment.'

Callie paced the small area of her hallway—the place where Finn had made love to her the night before. *Finn...* He'd made her better, she realised. Stronger. He'd left behind a little of his strength and a lot of his wisdom.

She could almost hear his deep voice in her ear. 'You don't have to accept or forgive her choices—just understand why she made them.'

Not now, she thought. *I'm still reeling because you're not here.*

'You can move mountains. You don't need her to be happy. And I'm still with you.'

He was, Callie realised. Oh, she missed him desperately, but he'd left a part of himself with her. His belief in her. She *could* move mountains, she *could* be happy—one day, maybe. She was stronger than she thought.

She could choose either to hang on to her bitterness towards her mother or she could set herself, and her mother free. She could listen to what she had to say and then decide whether she wanted Laura back in her life—*wanted*, not needed!

She might not be able to make a certain travel reporter

love her, but, by God, she could do this, she could face her mother.

Callie turned back to the door and wrenched it open. 'Come in and talk, but I'm making no promises beyond this meeting.'

Laura bit her lip as she stepped into the hall. 'I understand.' She glanced down, transfixed by the rings on Callie's hand. 'Oh, my goodness. You're wearing them! And on your wedding finger!'

'I'm not married,' Callie hastened to explain, lifting her hand. 'You *know* these rings?' she asked, confused.

'Sure. Your father bought them for me from an antique store to celebrate your birth.' Laura placed the tip of her finger on the raised stone. 'They were the only rings I ever wore.'

Callie looked up at the ceiling and let out a deep breath. Of course they were. Because this was her life and nothing could be simple.

It wasn't a surprise that Alaska in the dead of winter was cold, Finn thought, looking out from his hotel window into the weird light that was supposed to signal dusk—at two in the afternoon! In an hour or so it would be pitch-dark and the sun had only appeared four hours earlier. Crazy place, crazy life.

Fairbanks, Alaska, in the dead of winter and he was alone. Oh, the Northern Lights were amazing, awe-inspiring, incredible—all the adjectives so many writers before him had used and the ones he intended to avoid when he finally got around to writing his article. But his was a strange life, and one he wasn't sure he wanted any more.

He still hadn't turned in his honeymoon article and he wasn't sure when he would. Writing—always so easy—had become a task of herculean proportions. *Why?* His life, apart from no longer having a fiancée he seldom saw in it, was pretty much back to normal. He was back on the road, he had an editor squawking at him, and he was alone. So what was the problem?

He *liked* being alone, he reminded himself. Apart from his three weeks with Callie he'd always travelled alone and he was used to it. He didn't have to think of anyone, could jump into his work without distractions, didn't have to worry that he was neglecting anyone.

So, Einstein, if you like it so much then why are you feeling so damn miserable? Okay, he got that it was okay to miss Callie. They'd spent practically every minute together for most of the past month, so that was to be expected, wasn't it? He was allowed to miss her laugh, her piggy snores, waking up and realising that she was wrapped around him like a vine. And naturally he missed the sex. That was normal, right?

What *wasn't* normal was the crater-sized hole he felt in his heart at not seeing her again, not hearing that laugh, that piggy snore, not waking up to the feeling that he was being smothered.

This was the way he should have felt when he and Liz broke up, he thought. Wretched—as if the world had no colour, as if he was just going through the motions. Everything he should have experienced after losing his fiancée he was now experiencing in this cold, cold place on the other side of the world.

Was it just delayed reaction? Was he transferring his feelings for Liz on to Callie? He wished he was—it would help this crazy situation make a whole lot more sense. Unfortunately it had nothing to do with Liz and everything to do with that commitment-phobic wild-child woman he'd left behind in Cape Town.

He missed her…he wanted her. In his bed and in his life. Now and for ever.

That complicated and that simple.

He'd thought he could just walk away with a casual goodbye, with heartfelt thanks for helping him out of a jam and giving him the best short-term fling of his life. God, he was such a moron.

'What would you say if I said I was in love with you?'

Her memory drifted across his mind and he frowned, looking out into the nearly dark afternoon. Had she been trying to tell him something? Something crucial? At the time he'd just dismissed her cocky question as Callie being Callie, trying to push his buttons, teasing him as she often did. Then he remembered her serious eyes, the trepidation on her face that he'd ignored. Had he, in his quest to leave, to get back to normal, missed that she was trying to tell him that she loved him? That she wanted more?

In the dark, Finn moved to his laptop and moved his finger across the mouse pad, pulling up the folder named 'Angel'. Her face appeared on the screen and he stared at the images of her that changed every few seconds. Every photo he'd taken of her was filled with sunlight, with happiness, with joy. Everything his life didn't have now.

Finn shook his head. She was anti-commitment—she readily admitted to it. She thought that commitment and long-term were the emotional equivalent of the rabies virus. But she was also the woman who had resisted falling into bed with him, had tried to keep her distance because she'd said that she had the potential to fall for him. *Had* she? Fallen for him as he had for her?

Finn thought back on their relationship—to the glossy, sophisticated woman he'd first met and how her walls had slowly started to crumble. She'd begun to open herself up to him, to let him see glimpses of the lost little girl behind the charming, flirty façade. Finn knew that she wouldn't have done that for just any man, for just anyone. He'd got to her and she'd trusted him, let him look inside.

Trust was a very big deal for Callie...

Trust was a short degree of separation from love. For her and for him.

When Callie loved and trusted and decided to commit she'd do it with everything she had. He knew that without any hesitation. She'd toss her hat and every other of item of clothing she wore into the ring and go all out to make it work. She wouldn't cheat, she wouldn't run away, she wouldn't play games. She'd been hurt by love and she wouldn't want to hurt anyone *she* loved.

He remembered her question again. *What would you say if I said I was in love with you?*

I'd say I'm in love with you too, Cal, and call myself a million types of an idiot for not realising what you were trying to say earlier. I'd say my life without you isn't a life—it's just a random set of happenings that mean little.

I'd say I'm in love with you too...

Callie cursed Finn's lack of gardening skills as her shovel bounced off the hard soil in the corner of what had used to be a flowerbed. Didn't the man know that a garden required water? Pushing her hair off her sweaty forehead with the back of her hand, she looked at the shallow dent she'd made and sighed despondently.

This wasn't going to work. Oh, the bench looked stunning—a wooden three-seater, with a brass inscription screwed onto the back strut. Expensive, but worth the price—as was the case of beer she'd paid Finn's youngest stepbrother Michael so he'd let her onto the property and help her lug the bench into its position in the corner of Finn's yard overlooking the ocean.

To his credit, Michael had taken the crazy request from a strange woman in his stride and had refrained from asking too many questions. The ones he had asked she'd managed to fudge her way through.

Callie stood up and glared at the ground. She'd planned

to plant two rosebushes on either side of the bench, but now she thought she might take them away with her. There was no way they'd survive Finn's black thumb. Or lack of skill with a hose or a watering can.

Maybe she'd take them home and plant them in pots on her veranda—a reminder of the only man she'd ever loved.

She dropped the shovel to the hard soil and sat on the bench, resting her elbows on her thighs, thinking of Finn.

She could stay here for a while...hang out in his garden. After all, as she'd confirmed with Michael, he was still in Alaska and wasn't due home for a week or so. Then he was off to Patagonia—or was it Pakistan? She couldn't remember. But it didn't matter. He was away and she had time to deliver the bench, to plant the rose bushes—or *not* plant them as seemed to be the case.

God, she missed him. Missed everything about him.

They'd been apart two weeks and she still felt as if she was operating on only one cylinder, as if she was walking a tight wire. She'd tried to get back into the swing of things at work, taken a four-day trip to Milan, and had hated every second of it. Callie dropped her head and stared at the hard ground beneath her flip-flops. If her work didn't distract her from missing Finn then what was she going to do?

Go slowly mad? It was a very distinct possibility.

Man, life was just rolling on the floor laughing at her. Callie Hollis, party-girl and commitment-phobe, sitting on a bench, trespassing on her fake husband's—now *ex*-fake-husband's*—property and trying to keep from falling apart because she was ass-over-kettle in love with a man she'd promised not to fall in love with.

Yeah, life was such a joke.

Callie felt a tear drop off her chin and land on the hard-as-concrete soil below. Well, that was a hell of a way to get the ground wet. Finn had turned her into a crier—she'd never cried before he came along.

'Bastard...' she muttered, feeling as if that was the final insult.

'Sorry?'

At the deep, familiar voice Callie jerked her head up and whirled around. And there he was, standing a couple of feet behind her, dressed in board shorts and an old T-shirt, a four-day-old beard on his jaw. God, he looked good. *So* good.

'What are you doing here?' she demanded in a thready voice.

Finn's mouth kicked up, just a little, at the corners. 'I live here. What's your excuse? And why do I have a bench at the end of my garden?'

Suddenly Callie didn't know how to explain. Would he think she was sentimental? Sappy? That it was a stupid idea?

As he walked towards her she leaned back so that her shoulder was covering the plaque on the back of the bench. Would he think that she'd overstepped the mark? That she was being too presumptuous?

'Why the bench, Cal?'

'A view like this needs a bench,' Callie muttered, unable to meet his eye. He was now standing close enough for her to smell his aftershave, to feel the heat from his amazing body. She closed her eyes and told herself that she couldn't stand up and fold herself into his arms any more, that she didn't have the right to do that.

'There are chairs on the veranda with the same view,' Finn said, and Callie opened her eyes to see his strong hand—the same hand that had loved her with such skill—stroke the arm of the bench.

She wished he was stroking her. She'd reached a new low. She was jealous of an inanimate object.

'It's beautifully made. Hand-crafted?'

'Yeah.' Callie wished he'd take off his sunglasses. She needed to see his eyes because he had that implacable expression on his face. 'You needed a bench...'

'So you bought me one? OK.'

Finn walked around the bench and squatted in front of her. He shoved his glasses up into his hair and Callie sighed when her eyes met his. They were liquid and full of heat. God, she could look into those eyes for ever.

Finn lifted his hand and his thumb stroked her chin. 'You're filthy. Were you trying to plant these rosebushes?'

'You should water your garden more often,' Callie complained.

'I should.' Finn placed his hands on her knees and stared into her face, his eyes no longer playful. Instead they looked serious and intense. 'What are you doing here, Cal? Really?'

Callie hauled in air and scooted down the bench so that he could see the brass inscription. 'I wanted to do this for you. I thought you needed a place...somewhere to think about them.'

Finn looked at the inscription and Callie saw his Adam's apple bob.

'"In memory of James, big and small".' Finn read aloud.

He rubbed his hands over his face before staring at the plaque again. She couldn't tell what he was thinking and she needed to.

'If I've been too presumptuous or if you don't like it no harm, no foul. I'll take it away again,' Callie gabbled. 'I just wanted to give you some place where you could... I don't know...'

'Think about them? Remember them?'

'Yes...' Callie whispered.

'Thank you, angel.' Finn's voice was barely above a

whisper itself. 'It's spectacular. A little overwhelming, but spectacular.'

Finn reached out to rest his fingers on the inscription, his chest heaving under that ratty T-shirt.

After a little while, he looked at her again. 'How did you get in here? How did you get on to the property?'

Callie lifted a shoulder. 'Rowan had the email addresses for all your stepbrothers. Michael agreed to help me. He left about a half hour ago. He asked me to explain the "James, big and small" but I told him to ask you. That it was your story to tell. He said he would.'

'And he will. My brothers are insatiably curious.'

Callie winced. 'I'm sorry. I shouldn't have. I was out of line. I shouldn't have done this.'

Finn rested his hand on her knee and squeezed. 'No—thank you. It's an awesome gift. I'm at a loss for words, actually.'

Callie, thinking that this was a great time to go, abruptly stood up. The rosebushes would have to stay, she thought. Maybe Finn would plant them, maybe he wouldn't. She'd done all she could. It was past time for her to leave—before she broke down and begged him to let her stay.

Finn allowed her to stand up and watched her walk away, each step pulling her heart closer to breaking again. Why did he have to be here? Why couldn't she have done this without seeing him? It was taking every bit of will-power she had to put one foot in front of the other.

She was on the other side of the pool when he spoke again. 'Where are you going, Hollis?'

Callie turned back to look at him, standing tall and strong in the midday sunshine. She gestured to the house and shrugged. 'Home, I guess.'

'You guess wrong,' Finn told her, arms crossed. 'You're not going anywhere.'

She couldn't help the bloom of hope in her heart or the lifting of her chin at his arrogant words. 'Excuse me?'

'The only place you're going is into a shower. With me.'

Callie reached out and grabbed the back of a pool lounger to keep her balance, hope draining away. No, she couldn't do this. She wasn't going back to an affair, to crazy sex in the shower and then going home alone. She wanted more—she needed more. As much as she wanted Finn, settling for a no-strings, only-when-they-were-in-town-together fling would kill her.

Because she loved him so damn much.

'We can't go back, Finn.' She managed to croak the words out. 'I can't do it again.'

'Do what?'

'Have an affair with you!' Callie cried. 'I just can't—not again. Not feeling like this.'

Finn took two strides to reach her, and when he did he held her face in her hands. 'What are you feeling, angel? Tell me.'

'Why? What does it matter?' Callie flung the words into his face.

'It matters, darling Cal, because *you* matter.'

Finn brushed his lips against hers gently, briefly, before picking his head up and looking back into her shocked face. 'Okay, then, I'll tell you what *I'm* feeling. I saw you and my world settled down. I feel complete. Seeing you here makes me feel like I'm home. Normal.'

'Wha—at?' Callie frowned, confused.

'I came home from the gym, kicked off my trainers and walked onto my veranda—and I saw and heard you, cursing me for not watering my garden. And my world, for the first time in weeks, was the right way up. Me coming home, seeing you, made sense.'

'Um…what are you saying, Finn?'

Finn's smile warmed her from her toes up.

'I'm saying that I'm in love with you. Fathoms deep in love with you.'

'Oh.'

Finn's mouth twitched. 'That's all you've got?'

Callie held up her hand, trying to process what he'd just told her. 'You're in love with me?' she asked, just to clarify, not sure she'd heard him properly.

'Seems that way.'

Callie rested her forehead on his chest. 'Okay...wow.'

Finn's hand drifted down her spine. 'Still not the response I was waiting to hear. Any chance of *I love you, too, Finn*?'

Callie lifted her head and frowned at him. 'Of course I love you. How could you think for one moment that I don't?'

'Oh, let me think... Maybe it's the fact that you told me that you were going to use, abuse and toss me. That you aren't interested in commitment, that you don't believe in love, that I was allowed to seduce your body but not your mind.'

Finn rested his hands on Callie's hips and his forehead on hers.

'Might I remind you that you left me with that "Thanks for being a brilliant fake wife" comment?' Callie replied tartly.

Finn brushed his mouth across hers, sighed, and did it again. 'Okay, I admit it—we are equally bad at falling in love. Admitting we are in love. But I *do* love you. So much.'

Callie linked her arms around his neck and reached up to rest her mouth against his. 'I love you too.' She tipped her head back and her eyes laughed. 'So...what do we do now?'

Finn shrugged, his hand resting on her bottom. 'Haven't

the foggiest idea except that we go back to my original plan.'

'Which was…?'

His grin was pure mischief. 'You and me in the shower. Naked.'

Callie, her heart about to explode from happiness, thought that sounded like a marvellous idea and led him into the house.

The next morning Callie, dressed only in one of Finn's T-shirts, followed him through the garden to the bench, a cup of coffee in her wobbly hand.

Was this real? Any of it? Had they really made love all night long? Soft and sure, tender and wild, they'd lost themselves in each other's bodies, safe and secure in their love and their need for each other.

But what now? Where did they go from here?

Take a breath, Callie, she told herself. *Take it minute by minute, hour by hour. You don't need to have it all worked out right now. Right now you need to sit next to your man, on this bench, and watch the sea dance beneath the mid-morning sun.*

Callie leaned back against the arm of the bench and draped her legs across Finn's lap. He drew patterns on her bare thighs with his fingertips, his relaxed face lifted up to the sun. He was beautiful and he was hers.

'I spoke to my…to Laura,' she told him after watching him for a while.

Finn turned his head to smile at her. 'Yeah? And…?'

Callie shrugged. 'Old story. Married at eighteen, feeling like life had passed her by. Needed to leave to "find herself".' Callie lifted her cup to her lips. 'I don't know if we're ever going to have a mother-daughter relationship but I can be civil to her. *You* got me through that conversation, by the way.'

'I did? All the way from Alaska?'

'I heard you telling me you believed in me, that I could move mountains. You gave me your courage.'

Finn pulled a face. 'If I had any courage I wouldn't have left you and put us both through hell.'

'Maybe. But at least we realised that real life sucked without each other.' Callie put her cup on the arm of her chair. 'Talking about real life... How are we going to make this work? How are we going to be together? I know you don't want a long-distance relationship and neither do I.'

'Are you willing to give up your job?'

God, that was a big ask, but she would if she had to, as she told him. 'I love my job—I do. I wasn't sure I did six weeks ago, but having you in my life just makes everything seem exciting again.'

Finn's hand tightened on her knee. 'I would give up mine too, if it meant spending more time with you. So how about neither of us giving up anything?'

Callie's brows lifted. 'And how do we do that?'

'We travel together. If you're in London or Europe, I'll write about something in London or Europe. If you're in the States, the same thing. We spend most nights together. If there's an assignment I feel like I really need to take then it had better not take longer than a week—because that's my limit. That will always be my limit to the amount of time I can be away from you.'

Callie looked at him, astounded. 'Are you sure?'

'Hell, yes. What do you say?'

Callie bit her lip. 'What happens if one of us gets sick of travelling? What if I want to stay at home and—?'

Finn's eyes sharpened. 'And...?'

'Work in the garden? Redecorate the house?' Callie's voice dropped. 'Have a baby?'

Finn cupped her face with his hand. 'Then we both quit

and do something else. There'll always be something else, angel, but there's only one you and me.'

Callie took his hand and kissed the centre of his palm. 'There's only you for me.'

'Good to know.'

Finn glanced at her left hand and after Callie had explained why her dad had given the rings to her mother played with the rings with his fingers.

'You haven't taken them off.'

Callie felt her heart speed up. 'Should I?'

'Since I intend to change your status from fake wife to real wife as soon as possible, don't bother on my account,' Finn told her, his eyes blazing with love and passion. 'Proper proposal and new engagement ring to follow in due course.'

Callie gurgled with laughter. 'Just as long as you remember that I am trouble with a capital T. In neon letters.'

Finn sent her an amused look. 'I wouldn't have it any other way. Talent, as you once told me, shouldn't be wasted.'

* * * * *

Mills & Boon® Hardback

January 2015

ROMANCE

The Secret His Mistress Carried	Lynne Graham
Nine Months to Redeem Him	Jennie Lucas
Fonseca's Fury	Abby Green
The Russian's Ultimatum	Michelle Smart
To Sin with the Tycoon	Cathy Williams
The Last Heir of Monterrato	Andie Brock
Inherited by Her Enemy	Sara Craven
Sheikh's Desert Duty	Maisey Yates
The Honeymoon Arrangement	Joss Wood
Who's Calling the Shots?	Jennifer Rae
The Scandal Behind the Wedding	Bella Frances
The Bridegroom Wishlist	Tanya Wright
Taming the French Tycoon	Rebecca Winters
His Very Convenient Bride	Sophie Pembroke
The Heir's Unexpected Return	Jackie Braun
The Prince She Never Forgot	Scarlet Wilson
A Child to Bind Them	Lucy Clark
The Baby That Changed Her Life	Louisa Heaton

MEDICAL

How to Find a Man in Five Dates	Tina Beckett
Breaking Her No-Dating Rule	Amalie Berlin
It Happened One Night Shift	Amy Andrews
Tamed by Her Army Doc's Touch	Lucy Ryder